Once in a Lifetime

HARPER BLISS

OTHER HARPER BLISS BOOKS
Life in Bits (with T.B. Markinson)
A Swing at Love (with Caroline Bliss)
No Greater Love than Mine
Once Upon a Princess (with Clare Lydon)
In the Distance There Is Light
The Road to You
Far from the World We Know
Seasons of Love
Release the Stars
Once in a Lifetime
At the Water's Edge
The French Kissing Series
High Rise (The Complete Collection)

IN THE PINK BEAN SERIES
More Than Words
Crazy for You
Love Without Limits
No Other Love
Water Under Bridges
This Foreign Affair
Everything Between Us
Beneath the Surface
No Strings Attached

Copyright © 2015 by Harper Bliss
Cover design by Caroline Manchoulas
Published by Ladylit Publishing – a division of Q.P.S. Projects Limited - Hong Kong
ISBN-13 978-988-14204-5-9
All rights reserved. Unauthorised duplication is prohibited. This is a work of fiction. Any resemblance of characters to actual persons, living or dead, is purely coincidental.
No part of this book may be reproduced in any form or by any electronic or mechanical means, including information storage and retrieval systems, without written permission from the author, except for the use of brief quotations in a book review.

CHAPTER ONE

Jodie has always looked too damn glam to be a social worker. Look at her. She's only just gotten out of the shower, and already she seems to have this sheen to her. A sheen I used to find irresistible—all glossy and inviting and yes-I-will-let-you-do-that-to-me—but now it shrouds her in a distance I can't seem to bridge anymore. As if she's made her decision already.

On top of that, she knew I didn't want to come here. Not to Gerald's place, with all its man things, and a few of Troy's toys always lingering, no matter how many times the cleaner comes before we arrive for the weekend—I guess even people who get paid to tidy get tired of the never-ending task of stowing a child's toys.

Jodie has her arms wrapped around her body, clothed in the light-blue silk robe she always wears after taking a shower. She looks out over the beach, as if answers are there, in the sand that has been brushed clean overnight by the ocean. Answers to how to resolve this always-returning argument between us, the one that's been wearing us down for months.

"Hey," she says, finally, turning away from the window. "Did you manage to get some sleep?"

I wonder how I must look to her now. And how would Gerald feel about his ex-wife's partner sleeping on his Chesterfield sofa in nothing but a t-shirt and panties?

"Some." In the beginning, when Jodie and I had just gotten together, it was a thrill to come to her ex's lavish Hamptons beach house for a dirty weekend. But now, six years down the line, when she suggested coming here as a sort of last resort it felt more like she was trying to tell me something. The way she also does sometimes without words. Her face all brooding and unreadable, although I don't need to see her eyes anymore to know that it's over.

I could have slept in Gerald's room—or Troy's—but deciding to sleep on the sofa last night felt like a defiant stand. Now, in the cold hard light of day, it feels like a decision made by someone foolish enough to put stubbornness before a good night's sleep. At thirty-three, I'm not old by a long stretch, but, all the same, my bones prefer a soft bed.

It's only Saturday morning, and already we're in the middle of this fraught stand-off. How will we get through the next twenty-four hours without biting each other's heads off?

"Coffee?" Jodie asks. Her expression is not unfriendly but her face is not exactly folded into a peace-making one either. And I can't help myself. I suspect she's naked underneath that robe, and I still feel it—I still want her—but too many ugly words have passed between us and neither one of us knows how to take them back.

"Sure." I sit up straighter. Stare at the coffee table. I have to hand it to Gerald; he has excellent taste in furniture. If we got along better, I'd ask him where he got this table, as a way of making small talk and being civil and all that, but Gerald and I have been wrapped in a silent, mutually agreed upon mild hostility since we first met, and I never had the inclination to do anything about it. I'm not in a relationship with Gerald, so why bother?

"Can't you try a bit harder?" Jodie used to ask me in the beginning. "If not for me then at least for Troy's sake?" I can still see her shake her head at me. "You can be so ruthless sometimes."

"My mother is called Ruth," I would tell her. "And as long as she's alive, I will never be Ruth-less." The first few times I used that line Jodie actually giggled and dropped the subject.

I get up and sit at the breakfast bar, looking out over the ocean, which is savage this time of year, the waves loud and brash—the way I like it.

"The waves are like you," Jodie once said, "they never know when to stop. They just keep on going and going. The tide may retreat twice a day, but it always—always—comes back with full force."

"That analogy does not add up at all, Jodes," I'd said. "You're just babbling." And I had grabbed her, pushed her down on Gerald's sofa, and shown her what it was like to just keep on going while she looked out over those waves.

"What would you like to do today?" I ask. Her hand trembles a bit as she pours me a mug of coffee and she spills a few drops on the counter. Neither one of us cares.

Disappear, her face seems to say. It's so pale, it seems all pigment has drained from her body. Jodie's always pale, what with her Irish blood and skin, but I can tell this... phase we're going through has worn her out. If only it were just a *phase*. "Go for a walk, I guess." She actually shrugs when she says that, as if it doesn't matter anymore what we do. "Maybe have lunch at Gino's."

I shake my head before sipping. The coffee is strong, the way we both like it.

"What?" Jodie stopped bothering to keep the irritation out of her voice months ago.

"What are we even doing here?" I know she'll blame me again for actually saying something, but I can't stand this anymore. All the love I had for her, everything we've built between us over the years, is not enough anymore to bear this.

"You know why we're here."

I look up from my coffee. Try to find something inviting in her eyes. I come up empty. "It feels to me like we're here for one thing only." I pause, ignoring the nervous contractions in my stomach. Something I learned to do in my first year in court. It's harder to do when a relationship is at stake. "To break up."

Jodie's eyes narrow. "If *you* want to leave *me*. You're free to go."

I purse my lips together and nod in mock understanding, my chin going up and down in the most passive-aggressive way I can muster. "Sure. Because if this ends, of course I'll be the one leaving *you* and you will have nothing to do with that."

Jodie just sits there shaking her head. "I can't change you, Leigh," she says after a while. "I want what I want, and you want what you want." Her voice breaks a little. We've said these things to each other before—in different versions, with alternative words—a million times, as if they need to be said a certain number of times before a decision can actually be made. If we're waiting for the pain that comes with them to go away, we'll have to wait until that ocean outside freezes over.

"Let's get out of here." I don't want to stay in this house with her. I don't want to spend my weekend drowning in this tension and not finding my way to the surface. My lungs are full of spite and anger and resentment already. Maybe it's better for her if she can hate me. After all, I'm the bad one here. I'm the woman who has the audacity to go through life without any apparent desire for motherhood. "Or better yet. I'll go." *I'll pack up my things and be out of our apartment by the time you get home tomorrow evening*, I want to add, but I can't say the words. "It's time," I say instead.

That she doesn't burst into immediate, passionate protest is like a knife in my gut, but it's not as if this was ever going to be pain-free.

"I think it is, as well. This is killing us one day at a time." We don't look at each other. In my case, for fear of seeing something in her face, her demeanor, or anything else, that I could latch onto. And I'm tired of fighting. Of coming up with arguments that won't win her over, because some things are just how they are, and no reasoning stands up to them.

But can this really be how it ends? The pair of us drinking coffee in Gerald's house? After all the shouting has been done, and the harshest words have been spoken, can it just be this calm conclusion that we draw?

"Okay. I'll go." I don't get up though. How can I? How can I walk away from Jodie Whitehouse? The woman who has given me everything. Why can't I be a bit more accommodating? After all, I don't mind Troy being around. It's not as if I detest children. It's not as if Jodie expects me to become a full-time mother. But it feels as if I have to give up a crucial piece of myself to stay with her and honor her wishes. Her fierce desire to have another child clashes so ferociously with my own wishes and it's laying bare a fundamental difference between us—one that can't be overcome by a thousand conversations, or the best sex we ever had in our lives.

"Leigh." Her leg touches mine for a split second, but is gone before I even get the chance to register her touch properly. "I —" But Jodie has run out of words, too. We knew months ago that words wouldn't save us.

"It's fine." This time, I do get up. Gerald's place has floor heating, so I don't even get punished with cold tiles under my feet. On the surface, it may look like I'm walking away scot-free, all limbs intact, no skin broken. Beneath my ribs, though, my heart breaks because I know what I'm walking away from. I know all too well, yet, I can't stay. Because staying would only mean more of this, more of this chipping away at what we once had, at each other's confidence and essence. It has to stop sometime. It stops today. At 11.34 a.m. on Saturday, the twenty-second of April 2003. The day Leigh Sterling and Jodie Whitehouse cease being a couple.

And we were a good one. We had it, that unidentifiable chemistry, that boundless passion, the knowledge that we saw each other for who we were and that, just maybe, this might be forever. But it wasn't enough. And the mere fact that even a love like this, a love like ours, is not enough, scars my soul here and now. I head to Gerald's guest room—the room Jodie and I have always used—where I left my bag last night, just to pretend that there might be a possibility of us sleeping in it together.

I don't bother showering; just throw the few items that made it out of my bag back in, slip into a pair of jeans, a washed-out gray hoodie, and my trainers. I glance at the bed Jodie slept in. The sheets are twisted and the pillows scattered, indicating she had a rough night. Nights before break-ups usually are. It was a quick drive to get here last night, because no one goes to The Hamptons when the weather is gray and heavy like this, and the icy silence in the car was only broken by muffled radio voices and nostalgic songs from the oldies channel. I guess our break-up was already a done deal and coming here just a formality. As if we couldn't break up in our home, as though the many memories we made there would stop us. The sight of our bedroom door, some paint peeled off the upper right corner. The picture of us above the fireplace, of Jodie and me in Hawaii, when, perhaps for the last time, we looked immeasurably happy. I'd just left the D.A.'s office for Schmidt & Burke and we'd splashed out. Maybe I should never have left the District Attorney's office. Perhaps me crossing over to *the other side* was what kick-started this entire process.

But I know I'm only fooling myself. I know very well what has brought me here, bag in hand, ready to leave this weekend place where we never really belonged anyway. It's me, and the immutability of what I feel inside, of not being able to meet Jodie halfway in this—not even a quarter of the way really. I know what I'm walking away from, however, and it hurts so much I find it hard to put one foot in front of the other, to leave this room in which we haven't slept together for a very long time. We came here to talk, to smooth things out, or, at least, that's what we told ourselves. It's not as if we could say, "Hey, let's go to The Hamptons and finally get this break-up over with, shall we?"

But then I somehow find it in myself to start walking. I descend the stairs for the last time—because why would I ever come here again? Jodie is in her robe, her hands clasped around that coffee mug that should be empty by now. What do we do? How do we say our final goodbye? I can't just walk away. Not after six years with her. There needs to be a gesture of closure.

"This is it, then," Jodie says, fingers wound tightly around the mug. Outside, the wind howls, and I feel its echo in my heart. My heart wants to scream. I want to cry. But I need to hold it together, need to make it to the car in one piece.

"Will you be okay getting back?"

But Jodie is a public transport girl, and she can train her way out of anywhere. She nods. Why am I prolonging this agony? Her hair is almost dry now. I always envied how she can wear it long and never has to do anything to make it look fabulous. "It just dries into perfection," she used to say when she was feeling sassy.

Will she walk toward me? Or, because I'm the one who's doing *the leaving*, should I make a detour? I'm by the door already, but only because the stairs end there. Again, I'm frozen in my spot. Am I doing the right thing? I recognize this last question as panic. Last-minute nerves. Fear. What am I going to do without her? Without our apartment to go home to? Where am I going to stay? And what will she tell Troy when he gets back from Gerald's on Monday evening?

"Bye," Jodie says, her voice a dagger in my heart.

"Yeah." The way we're doing this stands in such stark contrast to how we were as a couple that, perhaps, it's fitting. Perhaps this is the only way.

I reach for the handle and open the door.

CHAPTER TWO

I watch the door for a long time after Leigh has let it close behind her. As if she might come back. Change her mind. Undo everything. As if, on the way to the car, on those few steps between the front door and the driveway, something magical has happened, and an idea that will save us has sparked in her brain. But we—Jodie and Leigh—are not to be saved. So, I just stand there, looking at a shut door. It's a beautiful one. Large in a classy, designer way, and shiny in... ah, hell, I don't know which tint of brown. All I know is that Gerald's money bought it and that Leigh never wanted to walk through it.

I'm still clasping my hands around this mug. I can't let go because it's the mug I drank from when we shared the last coffee of our life together. Everything I do now has this ring of finality to it. Or, if you look at it differently, of new beginnings. The start of my life without her.

Fuck, I love her. And I've let her go. Does she know how much I love her? How much she has changed me? Six years is hardly a lifetime, but it sure as hell feels that way now. And what am I going to do with myself, right now? I chose to come here to The Hamptons so I feel like I should stay.

I wait a few seconds longer but the door remains shut. I heard her car leave the driveway minutes ago. My wishful thinking is based on pure fantasy. And what if she did walk through the door again? I still couldn't take her back. The first thing that changes in this tableau vivant of *Broken-hearted Woman in The Hamptons* I imagine myself in, is the mug slipping from my fingers. As if all strength is draining from me and even an empty cup is too much to hold. It falls to the floor, but it doesn't break. It's empty, so there won't be any stains to wipe away either. My legs give out next. I crash to my knees—shattering the way the wretched coffee mug wouldn't—and I know I will have bruises, but what does it matter? Leigh is gone. Then the tears come in waves, like the ocean outside.

We didn't even hug. I can't even remember the last time we touched. Have I really become so cold that I let her leave without even the briefest of touches? Tears rain down on the floor, next to the unbroken mug. I try to wipe them with my robe, but silk is not very absorbent. Fuck, I scream on the inside. What have I done to us? Because Leigh might be the one who walked out, but I'm the one who made her do it.

Still, it's not as simple as that. I spread myself out on the floor in a dramatic fashion, arms wide, head to the side, as if I've fallen and can never get back up without the help of someone else. Without her.

I first saw her in court. I could tell she considered herself a bit of a hot-shot, even though her only task that afternoon was to sit there and observe. She'd only just joined the D.A.'s office, but I could already tell she was the kind of person who wouldn't keep on fighting the state's battles for the rest of her life. Even in a cheap pants suit, she had some glitz about her. Her hair was longer then, with sideways swept bangs that covered her eyes when she didn't brush them aside. She pushed her hair away from her face a lot that day.

After the court hearing, her colleague, Dan Mazlowski, quickly introduced us, but they both had other places to be. Leigh shook my hand with determination, like a woman who knew the importance of a strong handshake—like a woman working in a man's world. If I registered on her radar at all that day, she didn't let on. It would take five more weeks until we met next.

I saw her exiting the courthouse, coming down the steps with sure strides, as I made my way inside. She just nodded. I've always remembered that she wore pinstripes, and I considered that an odd choice. I only allowed myself a brief frivolous thought of another woman that day. I was still getting used to being a divorced woman, living in a small apartment on the Upper East Side, sharing custody of a child. My mind was overflowing with babysitter schedules and how to make my modest city paycheck last until the next payday. And there was Alexander to consider, the boy on whose behalf I was testifying that day.

The main reason for my divorce from Gerald was crystal clear to me, but I simply hadn't had the time to pursue anything. Nevertheless, despite our very brief introduction a few weeks earlier, and this quick, courteous nod on the steps, something did register with me. I didn't realize at the time, but looking back, I had to acknowledge that somewhere deep inside, I already knew I wanted to see her again.

The next time I saw her was at my office. There was that handshake again and I noticed for the first time how broad her hands were, as if slightly out of proportion with the rest of her. Her fingers were long, like her, but also wide, and so strong.

"I'm here for the Cindy Latimer case," she said, her brown eyes resting on me. "Good to see you again, Mrs. Dunn."

"Oh, it's Whitehouse. I guess my name change hasn't made it through all the channels yet."

She tipped her head a fraction to the right. "I guess not," she said, and only then let go of my hand.

"Please, call me Jodie." She was wearing pinstripes again. I escorted her to my cubicle, where we huddled so closely over a case file I could smell her perfume. I recognized it as DKNY, one of my personal favorites.

"I guess I'll see you in court then, Jodie," she said, a broad smile on her face. I felt it then. I didn't have much experience at picking women who were into women out of a crowd, but somehow, with Leigh Sterling, I knew. Built-in gaydar, perhaps. If only it had worked when I looked in the mirror before I married Gerald.

"I look forward to it." I extended my hand and suddenly I couldn't wait for her to take it in hers again. As she did, her smile transformed into a crooked grin.

"Poor word choice, perhaps," she offered. "Considering what happened to the girl on whose behalf you'll be testifying."

I was so taken aback, I didn't immediately know what to say. I still stood there, slightly entranced by this woman who opened up rather a few possibilities in my mind, that I could only mumble, "Sorry. Didn't mean to be unprofessional about it."

She gave my hand one last squeeze. "Day after tomorrow, then?"

"See you there." I watched her walk off.

"Earth to Jodie," Muriel in the cubicle next to me whispered. "Come back to us, please. The New York City Administration for Children's Services needs you. The children need you."

"Shut up," I hissed, feeling caught out.

"You're smitten." Muriel couldn't let it go.

I sat back down, hoping that disappearing from her sight would put a stop to her teasing.

"You don't giggle like that when Dan comes to see you, Jodie. And you especially don't stutter like that."

I wheeled my chair back so as to get a good look at her. "I wasn't stuttering."

"Hm-mm." Muriel rolled her eyes at me. "Sure, girl. Believe what you want. I'm just an innocent bystander, that's all."

"What do you think of her?"

"Of *her*?" She pursed her lips together. "Hot piece of ass, for sure. As for what I think of you, *Mizz* Whitehouse… I think you want a slice of that."

I shook my head. "Please, Muriel. Must you be so crass?" I said it in the voice I used to impersonate our supervisor.

"I must." Muriel stretched her legs and rested her feet on an overflowing trashcan. "I *must* also discuss this further with you over drinks after work."

"I can't tonight. I have Troy."

"Then you and Troy must come to dinner and we shall discuss this further while Francine helps him with his homework."

"He's five, Muriel. He doesn't have homework yet."

"Then she'll build a fort with him. Whatever. God knows the woman is broody and she loves that child. Do it for her." She tapped her thumbs together. "And you'd better know who to call to babysit when you and the sexy ADA go on a date."

The ringing of Muriel's phone interrupted our conversation. Before she picked up, she pointed her forefinger at me, as if to say that what she'd just proposed was non-negotiable.

Our first date happened weeks later. After the Cindy Latimer case, Leigh rushed to another appointment and we barely had a chance to say goodbye. A similar case put us back in court together, only this time Leigh didn't win and instead of being placed in a state facility for his protection, Joey Williams, the child in question, was sent back to his family.

"Drink?" was all she said.

It was October, and the city was cold and wet. I'd stepped in a puddle on the way over to court and one of my shoes was soaked. Troy was at his dad's and when I looked into Leigh's eyes to say "Yes, please" I already felt a little bit better about the unfairness of the system and its repercussions on Joey.

My instinct and Muriel both turned out to be correct. Not even fifteen minutes into our date, Leigh said, "Just so you know, Jodie, I'm into women and I like you."

"That's very forward." My heart was thumping beneath my thick woolen sweater.

"I mean," she continued, "I could be all coy about it. Throw out some feelers. Probe gently into your personal life, but after the afternoon we've had, I don't really have the energy for games like that."

I nodded pensively, as if mulling over what she'd just said, while really I'd been dreaming about a moment like this—in various degrees of hotness—for weeks. From the get-go, she was someone whose presence in my life, no matter how small and infrequent, I couldn't shake. It sat there, at the back of my mind, coming to the fore out of the blue, and often late at night when I couldn't sleep.

"Additionally," Leigh hadn't finished yet, "I get a rather distinct sort of vibe off you. I wouldn't be saying all of this if I didn't." She ended with a wide smile. One that shot straight through my flesh, to body parts untouched for years.

"Well." I looked into my glass of cheap wine. Despite its acid taste, it was nearly finished. "I guess I'd better buy another round then."

"I'd much rather do something else with you than sit here and get drunk," Leigh said.

"Like what?" I asked, already mesmerized by the twinkle in her eyes.

Her response came in the shape of another smile. She bit her bottom lip, and I wished my teeth were doing that to her.

. . .

I pull myself from the floor, avoid the view of the ocean, and go straight upstairs. I pull some clothes out of my overnight bag, and as I turn, I catch a glimpse of myself in the mirror. As expected, my eyes are red-rimmed, my skin blotched, my cheeks puffy. I can't help but wonder if I'm looking at a woman who has done the right thing. Because if it was right to let her go, then why does it hurt so much? Why this urge to undo? To go back? To sacrifice, now that it's too late?

But I'm a mother. First and foremost, I am Troy Dunn's mother, and I want another child. It was one of the first things I told Leigh six years ago. Nothing is more important to me than my child. And I will have another. Was she not listening when I said that? Because I said it often, and in a clear voice. Of course, I waited. I needed to know where things were going with her first. Needed Troy and her to get acquainted. Needed to build our life together first.

Judging from the woman looking back at me in the mirror, I've gone and destroyed that life together. Yet, despite the blistering pain, somewhere beneath my ribcage, a sense of relief builds. I'm free now. No more fights. No more energy wasted on trying to convince her that this may actually be something she wants as well. No more talking to deaf ears. I know what I want. I can see it so clearly. Troy and I in Central Park pushing a pram. The look on his face when I first bring his brother or sister home. The wonder in his eyes. The first time he realizes he's someone's big brother now.

Over the past year, those thoughts have become my fantasies much more than anything I wanted Leigh to do to me.

I push a finger into the pillowy flesh of my tear-stained cheek. These signs of heartbreak will fade away over time, as will the most acute pain. I'll pull myself together. Go for a walk on the beach alone. Return to the city tomorrow. Go to work the day after and pick Troy up from his dad's in the evening. I will hug him, and explain to him why Leigh couldn't stay with us, and then I will hug him some more—for both our benefit. And our life will go on without her, until it's not just me and Troy anymore, and we welcome a newborn baby into our home.

I nod resolutely at the woman in the mirror. Her eyes brighten a tad. Then I catch a glimpse of the bed behind me, the bed Leigh didn't even sleep in, and it hits me again that she's gone. For good.

CHAPTER THREE

When I arrived at our apartment on Saturday after the drive back from The Hamptons, I was in such a state, I'm surprised I managed to throw some spare panties in a suitcase. Ours was not an easily uproot-able life. I moved into Jodie's apartment on York Avenue not long after we got together. My place was bigger, but hers was rent-controlled and located only a few blocks from Gerald's townhouse on East 78th Street. The plan was to find a place together after I'd been with Schmidt & Burke for a while, but that never happened.

So, now, I feel like it's Jodie's bell I'm ringing. I can hardly still call it *ours*, not even in my head. She buzzes me up. She knows I'm coming to collect my things. I already know that I won't be able to move everything I want this time either. She'll just have to live with my stuff for a while longer, until I figure out a more permanent place to stay.

I don't knock immediately when I reach the front door of 3B, but the door opens anyway.

"Hey," Jodie says and gestures for me to come inside. It's

strange to have her do that while the key to this apartment still sits snugly in my pocket.

My heart sinks when I see the two suitcases and the couple of boxes she has piled up in a corner. She wants me out so badly she packed up my things.

"You've been busy." I head over to the boxes.

"Look, I know you wanted to see Troy, but he's staying over at Jake's after his soccer game."

"How is he?"

Jodie stops in her tracks and looks at me as if I have absolutely no right to inquire about the well-being of her son, a child I shared a home with for almost six years. "What do you want me to say, Leigh? That he misses you? That you leaving has him crying himself to sleep at night? Because, yes, that's what he does. You know he adores you and it hurts."

I bite back the tears. "I wish you'd stop saying that I'm leaving you." I lean against the boxes, looking for some sort of support. "Because, to me, it feels much more as if you're not giving me an option to stay."

Jodie holds up her hands. "Let's not do this again." Almost instantly, her arms go limp again, drooping by her side. She's not looking very glam today, despite the glossiness of that skirt she's wearing. "I can't."

"I want to say goodbye, Jodie. I want to see him."

"Of course. I'll set something up. I promise. Today, I just couldn't—" Jodie wrings her hands together.

"I understand." It's not as if I have any claims to make on her child.

"Where are you staying?" She struts to the couch and sits, not looking me in the eyes.

"At a colleague's." When I arrived back in the city on Saturday afternoon, I decided to call Sonja on a whim. Most likely because I was in dire need of some admiration.

"Not Sonja?" Jodie asks, the inflection in her tone indicating that she already knows the answer. And that I've just reached a whole new level of despicableness.

I just shrug. It's easy for her. She still has a home.

"I can't take all of this now." I point at the boxes and think of the rickety pull-out couch in Sonja's broom cupboard which doubles as a spare room. "I just came to get some essentials."

"You seem to have gotten by without them for the past week." In a way, it satisfies me that she's getting worked up because I'm staying at Sonja's. Perhaps it wasn't the most dignified choice, seeing as Sonja blatantly hit on me one time Jodie joined us for after-work drinks, but what's the point of caring about that now?

"Can we please get through this in a civilized manner, Jodes?" I sigh. "It's hard enough as it is." My mind flashes back to that night when Jodie met Sonja. Jodie sat there pouting like a wronged teenager, sulking with a martini glass in her hand, her back to me and the rest of my colleagues. After I'd let her stew for half an hour, I took her home and showed her how much room there was for another woman in my life. "No one takes it like you, Jodie," I'd said to her while ripping her panties off her. "And you know it."

She nods and rests her head on her upturned palm, fingers cradling her jaw. "This place is not exactly spacious either. Just… don't wait too long."

I try to find her eyes, but she doesn't let me. I suppose asking if we could, at some point, still be friends, is out of the question. "I won't." I turn to the suitcases. "Are my suits in here?"

"They're still in the closet. I wanted to leave them hanging up." And it's this mundane, homely piece of information that kills me the most. Because Jodie can't help but care about things like that, just as she can't leave any dishes in the sink before she goes to bed. Having my stuff linger here must be terrible for her, not just on a personal level, but it must seriously mess with her OCD.

"I'll just take those and the suitcases. I'll come back for the boxes as soon as I can." I can't begin to imagine what opening these boxes will do to me, knowing that she packed them.

"Okay." Suddenly, she stands. "Please, come here." Her voice has grown small.

I don't question it, just go to her.

"Just... one last hug. To say goodbye properly." Jodie's a few inches shorter than I and when she looks up at me like this, her eyes pleading and her lips trembling, I actually want to question my desire not to have children—again.

I wrap my arms around her. Her head presses against the flesh above my breast, as it has done countless times, and at first the embrace we stand in is strangely soothing, until wetness spreads where my blouse is open, and Jodie is sobbing, her tears hot against my skin.

"Hey." I curl my fingers around her neck, also a tried and tested gesture between us, and pull her up so I can look at her. I know this sucks, I want to say, but what the hell kind of difference will it make now? I wipe away some of her tears with the back of my hand, but it's pointless, because a gazillion more of them moisten my hand and her cheek, as if something has broken behind her eyes, something that, right now, looks like it can never be fixed again. So, instead of talking, I slant my head toward her, and I kiss her. Her lips taste salty and they are slippery, but she easily allows me access to her mouth. My tongue slides in and I try not to think of the circumstances. I try not to wonder about the uselessness of break-up sex. I'm not even sure I can do it. I'm not sure this can go further than this sloppy, wet kiss, which could be considered as part of that goodbye hug she asked for.

Or perhaps she was asking for more.

Jodie's lips are frantic on mine. She bites and sucks as if

there's no tomorrow. I can't blame her, of course, because for us, there is none. There's only now. One last moment. One last opportunity to be Jodie and Leigh. One last chance to change our minds, perhaps? But no, I think we both know that ship has sailed. This is just a way of saying goodbye, as opposed to the hurried manner in which I fled the house in The Hamptons.

Jodie's tugging at my shirt buttons already. Her mouth has descended to my neck. Her hands are on my belly, crawling upward, and her fingers slip under the underwire of my bra. I have no more time to question if I really want to do this. Jodie has decided for me. For once, I let her. We can have this. Even if it's just an instant during which we don't have to face the consequences of who we have become. Two people wanting vastly different things from life.

So I hoist Jodie's top up, and we unglue for a second, and I still can't find her eyes. She can fuck me, but she can't look at me. Somehow, I understand. Understanding each other was never an issue. We're both very good at laying out arguments, displaying logic, and making each other see why we want certain things. If only life's issues could be resolved by understanding each other.

Because I understand what Jodie needs now. She needs to forget. She needs a moment to hold onto, something between us to look back on other than all this pain we've caused each other. And right now, in the state we're in, this can only be physical.

Jodie doesn't wait for me to undo her bra. She rips it roughly off and throws it on the sofa behind her. She barely gives me the opportunity to take in her breasts one last time. Those tiny nipples of hers, that can grow hard just by being gazed upon. They're so pink and perfect, but there's no time to dwell. Jodie practically grabs me by the neck and shoves them in my mouth. She's not usually one to be so forceful, but that, too, I get. She wants to leave an impression, make a memory. And, perhaps, she also wants to make sure that, grief-stricken as I am, I don't end up in Sonja's bed.

Her mouth is by my ear and at first she just sighs and moans, but then she says, "Fuck me, Leigh." And if she wanted the hinges to come off, her wish has been granted. I move away from her breasts and let her nipple fall from between my lips.

"Look at me," I say, my voice demanding. "Look at me, Jodes."

Her eyes are still filled with tears and her cheeks are smeared with mascara.

"Take off your skirt." I hadn't noticed before, but it's the one we bought together a few months ago, during a weekend which we both firmly believed was to bring us closer together again. Because the human brain can trick you into believing anything if you really want it to. Is that why she wore it? It doesn't matter now. It's coming off, slipping into a puddle of dark-green fabric on the hardwood floor.

She's taken off her underwear as well and she stands before me naked. Quite the parting gift, I think, without a hint of cynicism.

I strip quickly and methodically before pulling her toward me because, as always, this is going to be my show. The one where I call the shots.

Together, we sink to the floor. Only part of it is carpeted, but it'll do. Jodie stretches out beneath me, her legs already spread. But some of the earlier frenzy has escaped us and the atmosphere is now morphing into a more solemn one, like a moment that needs to be cherished. If we rush this, we're lost forever. We will have spent our last moments on a quick orgasm built on heartbreak. I think we both know it can't be like that. Making a memory like that now would hurt too much, and everything is already so unbearably painful.

I lean over and kiss her. Slowly. Savoring her, although all I taste are salty tears. Our breasts press together in this final embrace, our nipples meeting in that way that can be so exciting. The way only being with another woman can feel. Softness on softness. Everywhere we touch, pillowy curves and smooth skin. It's what Jodie said to me after our first night together. "I can't believe how soft it is," she'd said, and it had made me laugh, although it was true, but she was just so damn cute when she said it, as if it was the biggest revelation of her life. Maybe it was.

While I kiss her I let a hand roam down her belly. I wonder how many fingers would be appropriate for a goodbye fuck. I can't give her less than three, but all five seems too much for the occasion. Too intimate.

"Fuck me," Jodie says again, her hands in my hair. And then I do. I let three fingers slither through a wetness that baffles me. Then again, it always has, and it's almost cruel that even now, during our very last moment together, it still does.

And it still turns me on as much as it did the first time I let my fingers wander between her legs. And this time, she gazes back, she stares up at me, and I know what that look means, because I know Jodie better than anyone does, and, especially in these circumstances, I know her better than I've known anyone in my life. She wants more. That's what the non-blinking is about. The open mouth with no words coming out. Because I can't give her anything else anymore—and, more particularly, the very thing she wants most in life, more than me—I give it to her.

I push three fingers inside of her, but quickly follow up with a fourth. To be inside of her after such a long time, because the past six months we spent most of our private time either in fraught arguments or in cold, distant silence, makes me well up. I can't help it. The sob starts in the pit of my stomach, engaging my entire body. Because I'm fucking Jodie. I can feel my clit throb between my own legs, and this might be the most painful fuck I've ever been a part of. There's pain, and more pain, but also the look of longing in Jodie's eyes. Those beautiful green eyes, which were probably the first thing I noticed about her that time, so long ago when we were introduced at the courthouse. Green eyes are so rare, so of course they captured my attention. And I liked what I saw. I still do. Even though a mist of tears clouds them and our faces are so close my own tears add to the wetness of Jodie's face, and I can't see them right now. And then I realize that what we're doing right now is just as messy as what we've become. We're lovers who will turn into exes, perhaps even strangers.

I'm inside a woman who will disappear from my life. A woman I've loved for six years. A woman who opened herself up to me in ways we both deemed unimaginable when we first met.

"Oh Leigh," Jodie moans, in that way of hers, and this is a million times more painful than when I walked out of the door at the house in The Hamptons. But maybe we need this pain. Because how else could we possibly mark the end of our affair than with regret in our hearts and tears in our eyes?

Then she comes for me for the very last time, and I can feel her climax shudder through me, like a parting gift. And then, it's over. Then we're just two naked people on our—her—apartment floor, trying to wrap their heads around what just happened, and quickly realizing that nothing has changed. I still need to drag my suitcases down the stairs and leave.

CHAPTER FOUR

My alarm clock is one that Leigh bought. She'd broken the one I'd had for years after slapping it with all her might one too many times. She was never much of a morning person. And now I'm stuck with it. It sits there, during the night when I can't sleep, its red digits mocking me. I should have put it in one of her boxes. I still can. She left them. I'll never know if that's because she still wanted to leave a piece of herself in our apartment, or if she genuinely didn't know what to do with them. And if she thinks it's easier for me because the lease on this apartment is in my name, she can think again. Even with most of her things packed up, her presence is everywhere.

Not for the first time, I wonder if this agony is worth it. But I can also hear Leigh's words in my head: "We're fundamentally different people, Jodie," she said, in the aftermath of one of our fights, after we'd calmed down enough to use a normal tone of voice again. "Perhaps, if our differences were about something less important than the desire to procreate, we could maneuver around them, but this… it's too big for negotiations and compromise. The last thing I want is to make you unhappy. If I stay, that's what will happen."

When she first said it, I still believed I could change her mind. That my love was powerful enough to accomplish that. That was my mistake. Perhaps I should have run at the first sign of our incompatibility.

"Do you want children?" I asked over a breakfast of mimosas and croissants. We sat half-dressed on Leigh's sofa after one of our early dates and a wild, wild night that had left me so dazed and satisfied, her reply didn't even matter at that point. I was just thinking of Troy, the way I always did after waking up.

Leigh put her mug on the coffee table and reached for her champagne flute. "Can't say that I do."

I was so smitten her words barely registered, even though, somewhere in the back of my mind, a red flag was being raised nonetheless. But this was our third date, so not exactly the time to plan how many kids you see yourself having. But there was no hesitation in her voice when she said it, only determination.

"Is that a deal breaker?" she asked.

"Well, you know I have a son." Troy was at Muriel and Francine's, most likely being spoilt rotten.

Leigh smiled the sort of smile that could make the more susceptible kind of judge melt on their bench. "Whom I would love to meet." She locked her big brown eyes on mine. She'd slipped into the silk blouse she'd worn the night before, but hadn't buttoned it properly, and it had slid off one shoulder. Those shoulders. I could look at them for days. "But I don't want any of my own."

It was more than enough to placate me at the time. "Maybe we can pick him up together later?"

Leigh nodded thoughtfully. "As long as later means I get to do this now." She disposed of her glass and reached for my legs, pulled me toward her and flattened me on the sofa. The first year of our relationship, we didn't spend a lot of time talking. She fucked me again then, and not even in the way that would change me forever.

The first time Leigh really took my breath away, we'd stayed in at my place during a weekend that Troy was at Gerald's.

"Why go out?" Leigh had asked when she'd arrived. "When there's plenty to do in the comfort of your home?"

I was sure my eyes had started glittering with anticipation, but I only saw Leigh's eyes when she said it, and something I couldn't place shone in them. A darkness I hadn't yet encountered. It ignited a yearning in my belly I'd never felt before.

She barged her way in, shut the door behind her, and with subtle but clearly noticeable force, shoved me against it. She looked into my eyes, waiting for some sort of approval, but I was already too aroused to give her that. The stupid grin on my face was probably enough for a woman like Leigh to understand that she was on the right track.

Slowly, she trailed her fingers along my arms, only to snap them around my wrists hard, denting skin. She hoisted my arms above my head and pinned my wrists to the door with those strong fingers of hers. All the while, her lips sported a grueling, sneering sort of smile that left me wet like a river. It was as if what I had seen in her the first time we met, what I had seen flash in her eyes, that unquantifiable spark that had passed between us that I had mistaken for gaydar, was actually something else entirely. A sort of recognition, perhaps, an unexpected encounter of kindred souls.

She didn't say anything, just looked at me, giving the impression that a few glances were enough to read the entirety of my being, my desires, what—bone-deep—I really longed for.

That sneer told me that she had it all figured out, and the wordlessness of it was the biggest turn-on of all.

One hand grabbed my wrists in a tight grasp while the other unbuttoned my jeans. No kisses, and certainly no displays of tenderness, were exchanged before she slipped her fingers all the way into my panties and caught my already swollen clit between two digits, pressing hard.

My breath caught in my throat, my knees giving a little.

Then, she broke eye-contact and brought her lips to my ear. "Here's what's going to happen, Jodie," she said, her voice all command. "I'm going to fuck you against this door and you're going to come for me. Don't make me wait for it, or else…" She released my clit, and the walls of my cunt clenched around nothing. Not for long, however, because one of her fingers was already sneaking closer.

Leigh dug her hand deeper into my pants, her wrist rubbing against my clit as she sought entrance to my cunt. She jammed her fingers inside in a rugged manner while her teeth sank into my earlobe. The fingernails of her other hand dug into my palms as—there's really no other way to describe it—she took possession of me. And I knew, there and then, that nothing else would ever do for me again. This was it. Nothing I, or even we, had ever done together had impacted me so profoundly. Because it wasn't pain I felt. It was something beyond pain, something beyond physical awareness, like a life-long thirst in my soul being quenched.

All my senses stood to attention as Leigh fucked me. This was not making love, as Leigh would later point out. This was fucking, and the fire in her glance when she said it left no room for contesting. Her DKNY scent filled my nose, and her teeth kept biting, rhythmically, and her fingers kept delving, and I was spread so wide, and filled to the brim, that I had no idea how many fingers she was using, but what turned me on the most was the immobilization of my hands, the sense of surrender that came with her controlling me in that way. What she'd asked of me earlier, came easily, although I was quite curious about the 'or else' she had threatened me with.

She must have known I was about to come and brought her face back across from mine to glare at me. She pushed harder with both hands, pinning my wrists painfully to the door, probably leaving bruises, while down below, she seemed to take hold of me, of everything of me, my pussy the entrance to the core of my being. She was in charge of everything.

My brain went blank as the climax momentarily paralyzed my limbs. Leigh pushed her body against mine to keep me upright, otherwise I would surely have crashed to my knees, weeping, as if this was my first time coming at her hands.

When I came back to my senses, her lips were on my neck, and both her hands in my hair. I remembered how I'd said to her the first time we had sex that I was blown away by the softness of it. Maybe that had inspired her to try something else because there was nothing soft about what she'd just done to me.

"This is just the beginning," she whispered, her lips on my cheek. "Just an introduction, Jodie." And only then did she kiss me.

I toss and turn in the faint red light of the alarm clock. I'm not wondering where and when I'll ever find a woman like Leigh again. I know I won't. I don't want to, either. I had the passionate, all-effacing love affair. Now it's time for something else. A visit to my ob-gyn, for starters. I'm thirty-six. If I'm lucky, I have more years for this, but now feels like the right time. If I can't have both Leigh in my life and another child, I'll choose another child. For the longest time, I held on to the belief that I would never have to choose, that life would arrange it so it would never have to come to that. But here I am. Alone in bed.

Leigh's side unoccupied from now on. Because I can't possibly imagine another woman taking her place in my bed. Not because we only just broke up, but simply because I can't envision another woman doing what she did to me.

At the first light of dawn, I can't bear to be in the apartment on my own anymore. I take a shower and go for a walk. My plan is to keep walking until the hour is decent enough for me to pick up Troy from his friend's house. I need desperately to spend every minute of this day with my son. Life always goes on when you have children. When you have someone to take care of.

"Up at the crack of dawn." I hear a voice behind me. I don't need to turn around to know that it's George from 4A. "Are you sleeping like us old codgers now?"

I wait for him to catch up with me. He's probably gone around the block a few times already. It's what he does to pass the empty hours of his life. His words, not mine.

"Just going to fetch Troy." It's not a lie and I don't feel like getting into the real reason behind my early Sunday morning walk.

"Missus having a lie-in?" He cocks his head like he's asking about a secret between us. As if Leigh hasn't lived in the same building as him for the past five years, carried his groceries up the stairs, and even watched baseball games with him on his tiny, old TV. As if she only moved in yesterday, and it is still news-worthy that I am shacking up with another woman.

"She left," I blurt out. "She's gone. It's over." It comes out in a rush of short words, like something that really needs to be said. As though saying it to George equals announcing it to the world.

"Oh, dear." George leans on his walking stick a bit more,

like he's the one who needs the most support. "I sure am sorry to hear that."

Not as sorry as I am, I think. But sorry is not the right word. A car swooshes past us, obviously over the speed limit, and this would normally snag George's attention, but he doesn't even bat an eyelid.

"Are you okay?" he asks, and this old man asking about my emotional well-being shakes me again.

"Not really. But I will be." I catch a sly tear that has escaped with my thumb.

"Anything you need. I mean it." He stomps his cane, as if his voice alone is not enough to make the point. "If you need some quiet time when you have the little fella, let me know. I'll look after him. He loves my model plane collection. Can play with it for hours."

"Thanks," I say, and it suddenly hits me that, although Gerald and I share equal custody of Troy, and I've never really been a single mother, that's kind of what it feels like now. Me and my child against the lonely world Leigh left us in. Gerald and I had only been divorced a few months when I met Leigh. When she came swooping in and, so quickly, became a massive part of our lives. "I may take you up on that."

"Any time," George says. He tips his forehead with his fingertips. "I'll leave you to your business now."

I watch him wander off and it feels like all I've done of late is watch people walk away from me.

CHAPTER FIVE

Six months after Jodie and I broke up I jump at the chance of trading New York for San Francisco. Everything in New York reminds me of her, especially in October. We met in October and I can't seem to separate the month from all the first times we shared during it.

I don't care that I've only just settled into my new midtown apartment. That I only found the strength two weeks ago to unpack the last of the boxes that, in the end, remained in a corner of Jodie's apartment for months. When the offer from my firm comes to join the new office on the west coast, I don't hesitate. I grab the opportunity to leave with both hands.

Because I need to start over. I crave new surroundings. A clean slate. Soon the ice skating rink will be up in front of Rockefeller and I won't be able to walk past it without memories of Troy's and Jodie's gleeful smiles at my attempts to venture onto the ice with them. How Troy put his tiny, gloved hand in mine and said, "Come on, Leigh. I'll teach you." And how even a genuine, beautiful gesture like that wasn't able to sway me. For I fell in love with Jodie's son too. My heart is not made of stone and ambition alone. I loved Troy, but as soon as

Jodie started talking about another child, something in my brain failed to compute.

By the time the New Year rolls along, I'll be on the other coast. Maybe Jodie will be pregnant by then. Who knows? We have gathered mutual friends and acquaintances over the years, of course, but, as if they've all secretly agreed on the best strategy, they never mention my ex when we meet up, not intentionally anyway.

Granted, it was awkward when I ran into Muriel and Francine at the Chelsea Market a few weeks ago. Sonja had looped her arm through mine and I guess someone not in the know could have mistaken us for lovers, which we were, sort of, but it was all very lackluster on my side, a fact which Sonja didn't seem to care much about. All I could think when Muriel and Francine appeared in my line of vision was, *please don't let them see me* and *please don't let them draw the obvious conclusion and tell Jodie*. Then I was ashamed that I even had the audacity to think of Sonja that way. Sonja who had only been good to me, who'd given me a place to stay, and a shoulder to cry on. It remains unclear who actually took advantage of whom. I guess we're both guilty.

But they're not blind and Muriel has an inclination to latch on to other people's drama, so she swept us up and the four of us ended up in one of those trendy places in the Meat Packing District.

Muriel, one of Jodie's closest friends and someone she sees at work every day, apparently couldn't help but look at me disapprovingly, as if to say, "You've moved on quick enough." But she didn't know that I hadn't moved on at all. That leaving Jodie was far and away the hardest thing I'd done in my life, and that I doubted the validity of my decision every single day. Especially, too, during those long dark nights, when Sonja lay purring beside me, and I would drift off into slumber only to wake up again and again to find that the person next to me was not the one I wanted it to be.

"Please excuse me," I said. "I'm going to find the washroom."

"I'll go with you," Muriel cooed, right on cue.

As soon as we reached the bathroom, fitted out in nothing but ostentatious black marble, I cornered her. "It's not what you think."

"No matter what I think," she said, squaring her shoulders. "But let me tell you this." She brought her hands to her sides matron-like. "Jodie is in pieces and it's a good thing she has Troy because he's the only one getting her through this. So, if you're in any mind to reconsider, please do."

I knew she was forward, but I had never realized quite how much until then. "It's complicated," was all I could say.

"Hm-mm." Muriel shook her head dramatically. "Not in my eyes, it's not. She loves you and you love her. What's the problem?"

"Really?" I narrowed my eyes, gearing up for a fight. It had been a while since I'd had a good one in court. Maybe in her naiveté Muriel was trying to help, but she wasn't doing a very good job of it, and I could do without the lecture. "That's the line you're spinning me? How long did it take you to come up with that?" Muriel was at least two heads shorter than me and I used my height to my advantage by towering over her. "You're her best friend. You should know better."

"Listen, Miss Fancy Lawyer who has it all figured out." She didn't back down an inch. "Have you perhaps considered—you know, with that academic brain of yours—that what was valid six months ago may have changed? A break-up changes people. Shifts their perspective. Makes them see things differently and rethink their goals."

"Wh—what are you saying?" Suddenly, my heart was thumping wildly. "Has Jodie said anything?"

"It's really not for me to put words in her mouth, just… get in touch." With that, she turned on her heel and headed toward a stall.

"Muriel," I called after her. "Please don't tell her about Sonja. It's really nothing. We're colleagues and I've been staying with her, that's all."

"Oh, I know all about Sonja." She pushed open the door of the stall and disappeared.

I steadied myself against the wash basin, peering at my reflection in the mirror. Outwardly, our break-up had definitely changed me. My cheekbones were as sharp as in my teens, my eyes sunken deep into my face from lack of decent sleep, my skin grayish from too much booze. Looking back at me was a wreck of a woman. And then there were Muriel's words. Should I get in touch? Did Muriel mean that Jodie's wish to add another member to her family of two had waned?

I contemplated calling her every day after that washroom conversation with Muriel, but a week later the offer for San Francisco came in. It was not that I didn't love Jodie enough to check in with her and the status of her wishes—it was that I loved her too much. And I couldn't do it again. Couldn't give in to what might turn out to be false hope. My heart hadn't yet mended from when it was torn out of my chest after our first break-up. What if we ended up on her living room floor again, and I had to walk away all over again?

Muriel might be her best friend, but yet that didn't mean she knew Jodie better than I did. I knew the dark cavities of Jodie's psyche. I knew what she craved and what she could and couldn't say. I could read her, and, even though a part of me wished it hadn't, the past year *had* happened. That year in which we'd danced around the subject, playfully at first, until there was no more room for play, nor joy, because I couldn't picture myself walking, living, and waking up next to a heavily pregnant woman, not even if that woman was Jodie Whitehouse. A woman with a teenage son, a newborn on the way—both equally important to her—and me, trailing behind.

It wasn't only the absence of maternal instinct, nor the focus I put on my career—although they were the main reasons—that drove us apart in the end. For me, Jodie always came first. She had done from that evening in the bar around the corner from the courthouse in 1996. I even passed up on a faster track to my career goal to spend time with Troy when the babysitter bailed or something else came up, because I always enjoyed my time with him—even when it didn't fit my schedule. But I had to draw the line somewhere because if I didn't, where would that leave me in Jodie's life?

I witnessed first-hand, and on more than one occasion, how motherhood so fundamentally changed the lives of women whose ambition equalled mine during law school—former peers who, because of time constraints and shifted focus, are no longer a part of my life. It was as if they'd had a personality transplant. As if a switch in their brain had been flicked as soon as they gave birth, and all their previous, often loudly vocalized goals and dreams took an immediate and permanent backseat to their new role as a mother. A sudden transformation my logical brain can fully grasp, even though it was never something I wanted for myself. Not even with Jodie.

So here I am, on the first of many flights from New York to San Francisco. My boss, Steve, told me I'd most likely be flying over there every other week, until I move permanently by the end of the year. Perhaps it could be seen as another cowardly move on my part—as running away—but I know that only distance can heal that hole in my heart. Bumping into Muriel made that perfectly clear. Because what if I had run into Jodie? Or Troy? What would that have done to my heart? New York City is a huge city, but it's not big enough for my pain.

Sonja knew she had to let me go when I told her. At first, I was afraid she'd convince someone at the firm to let her relocate as well, but as it turns out she's not that besotted with me, after all. And New York is threaded through the fabric of her being too much. She can't leave it, not even for me. Not that I want her to.

The first night I allowed her to slip into my makeshift bed in her spare room, all I did was throw my arms around her and cry on her shoulder, cry until I believed I was empty, until the next night, the tears came again. That's what Sonja did for me. She let me cry, my tears gathering on her skin, wrinkling it, until I ran out. Until I was dry. Then we had sex a few times, but to me, it felt like encountering a trickle of water in the desert when all I was used to with Jodie were shattering, uncompromising waves of the wildest ocean.

When the plane touches down, I inhale deeply. I'm ready for my new life. The arm of the passenger next to me bumps into mine as she finally relaxes. Clearly, this woman is no fan of flying, just like Jodie, who always held on to me for dear life when we flew somewhere. I'd try to distract her by whispering silly things in her ear, making her laugh, or playing one of our favorite games.

Our last trip together was to Hawaii. We had an early morning flight back to New York and had gone on a massive bender the night before. I usually don't break a sweat while flying, but lots of turbulence and a martini hangover made even me shaky. Jodie, the sweetest person I've ever known in my life, took my hand in hers on that flight, brought her mouth to my ear, and whispered, "Tell me what you're thinking right now." The memory of that moment sparks another. Of the very first time I asked her that question.

"Tell me what you're thinking right now," I asked. We'd gone for a quick dinner at a restaurant around the corner from her apartment after dropping off Troy at Gerald's. I was cradling a glass of wine in my hands and Jodie kept staring at it.

"Don't think about it. Just say it," I urged. "Just blurt out whatever's going through your mind."

"Those hands of yours." Her voice had dropped into a lower register I could barely hear over the restaurant murmurs around us. "I wonder what else they can do."

I know she didn't mean spanking. We'd successfully graduated to that not long after I had pushed her against her apartment door on our seventh date. This was our tenth. I knew what she meant. "I'll show you." I swallowed a lump in my throat and called the waiter for the check. I couldn't get out of there fast enough. On our way to York Avenue, her shorter legs could barely keep up with me. But a fire in my belly had been stoked. I had considered it before, of course, as a natural progression of the sexual dynamic that was unfolding between us, and it was on the schedule, so to speak, but I definitely hadn't had any plans toward it on that particular night. In my mind, it was still much too soon. In the beginning of our relationship, reading Jodie, gauging her desires, was still very much a careful balancing act, even though I made it out as anything but.

"I want it all," Jodie said, as soon as we fell through the door of her apartment, and she pulled me close.

"You've got it." I injected a shot of bravado into my voice I didn't really feel. The prospect was exciting—almost unbearably so—but when someone asks that of you, it always comes with a burden of responsibility. Also, by then, Jodie was not just *someone* to me. The fire that crackled between us every time we met left me with more than growing desires and that ever-present wish to push boundaries. I was in love with her. We stood at the beginning of our journey together—a long and rewarding one, I hoped—and I didn't want to screw that up by making a false move.

Our kiss grew frantic in no time, our teeth breaking skin, until I pulled away and stared at her, until the silence around us became too loud. "Take off all your clothes," I commanded.

She did as she was told. It was a Saturday so she was dressed casually in jeans and a sweater. The way she stepped out of them indicated that she'd been waiting for this moment much longer than I could have suspected. The enthusiasm in her demeanor soon exterminated my nerves, because that was the thing with me and Jodie. We fed off each other's energy all the time. It was all cause and consequence. Sometimes it felt like a perfectly choreographed ballet of movements, intentions, and desires. It was the way it always clicked for us in the bedroom, the way we erased each other's doubts and got to the essence so effortlessly.

"On the bed." I stripped off my own clothes and followed her to the bedroom. There could be no disparity in the state of undress between us for this. We had to meet on a level playing field. The beauty of our give-and-take was always the equality in it. I never made her do things, I merely unearthed them from her psyche and then we did them together.

"Spread your legs," I said.

I moved onto the bed and sat between her legs, looking at what lay in front of me, mesmerized by the sight. I doubled-down in front of her and licked her wet pussy lips until she almost came. I could easily tell by the rapidly increasing twitches in her legs, which she pressed against my ears when I went down on her—unless I told her not to.

Then I stopped and pushed myself up so that I could see her eyes. She didn't say anything, but I felt electricity zing in the air between us. She let her knees fall open, spreading herself wide for me again, her breath coming in labored gusts. Clearly, she was on the edge of climax, and I was right there with her. Only, this time, we would go about it a bit differently.

I only looked away from her briefly to bring my hand in

position, and my eyes were back on hers when I let the first three fingers slip in. By then, three fingers was our standard. Nothing less, nothing more.

"Oh christ," Jodie murmured after the first stroke, her head falling back a bit, but not breaking eye-contact. I could still see it in her eyes. She was begging for more.

Adding the fourth finger was a mere matter of transition. She took it easily, as if she was used to it. Her pelvis gyrated, her pussy swallowed, enveloping my fingers in exquisite warmth.

"Yeah," she started saying then. "Oh yeah." Her hands had curled into fists, clenching the sheets between tight fingers.

I eased back and inched my thumb closer to the tips of my other fingers and spread her wider. I didn't go deep at first, let her get used to the changed shape of my hand, caused by only the slightest of alteration on my part, but making a world of difference for her.

"I want it all." She repeated what she'd said before, but now her voice was drenched in lust, and low with animalistic want.

Slowly, slowly, I let my knuckles touch the rim of her pussy, seeking entrance. It was the most I'd asked of her. I had to avert my gaze from her face and examine what my hand was doing. I watched as my knuckles slid over the entrance, and then all the way inside.

Jodie lay completely still, the movements of her pelvis having ground to a complete halt. It was all me now. I kept my hand immobile for a few seconds and reveled in this moment of complete surrender. I felt it burn throughout my flesh, underneath my skin, like the biggest, most immersive present anyone had ever given me. It was.

Then I started fucking her, the knuckle of my thumb sliding in as well, and to have someone spread so wide for you feels more like a spiritual experience than anything else. My clit swelled between my legs and I could feel moisture gather on my inner thighs, that's how wet I was.

I scanned Jodie's face. Her eyes were shut, her features a mask of concentration and utter bliss. And it had all started with a simple question: *Tell me what you're thinking right now.* Then her lips parted, but no sound came from her mouth. All the while, I shifted my hand inside of her with minute movements. This wasn't about motion so much as it was about being inside of her to such an extent it made both of our hearts explode.

Even though my task at hand wasn't strenuous, beads of sweat pearled on my forehead. This was a meeting of the emotional and the physical, and it was taking all I had.

"Oh Leigh," she said then, breaking the silence around us, and how she said my name chased a chill of pleasure up my spine. "Oh… Oh… Oooh."

Her entire body contracted around my fist. Jodie threw her head into the pillows and her fists uncurled, then curled back up again. That was the first time I witnessed someone totally surrender, to the moment, the action, the intimacy, and the feelings that blossomed between us. A new bar was set.

Ever so gently, I slid my hand out of her. I looked at it incredulously for an instant, as if I could hardly believe what it had just done, but then Jodie called for me, and I clearly remember the single salty line that a tear tracked down my cheek as I folded over her to kiss her.

CHAPTER SIX

From the moment my ob-gyn confirms I'm pregnant with a girl, I know I want to call her Rosie. Not Rose, or Rosamund, or Rosalyn, but just Rosie. Rosie Whitehouse. My dream come true.

My friends, Ginny and Susan, who had put me in touch with their fertility specialist and accompanied me on my first appointment, had warned me about the path of hope and disappointment artificial insemination would take me on. They'd had to try—and pay for—four inseminations before Ginny had gotten pregnant and successfully carried the baby to term. But, as if the universe knew I was more than ready—and that I had already sacrificed greatly—my very first insemination took, despite the odds being small. Dr. Barkin confirmed my pregnancy, monitored me closely, behaved moderately optimistic but always with an edge of caution to her words and demeanor, until I was in the second trimester and she gave me the go-ahead to start telling people.

Gerald is not necessarily the first person I want to impart the news to, but I'm so elated, so completely over the moon and buzzing with excitement, that I just blurt it out when I go to fetch Troy.

I see my beautiful boy who's growing up so fast and I'm so overwhelmed by love and hormones and joy, that I crouch down next to him, pull him to me, and say, "Guess what, handsome? You're going to be someone's big brother in six months' time." Gerald stands behind him and almost shrieks.

"For real?" he asks. "Oh, Jodie." From where I'm kneeling, his voice sounds teary. Gerald is a tall, broad, dark-haired man. Our marriage suffered from many more issues than my growing attraction to women and, to his credit, he never felt the need to blame it all on me. Always a cordial, well-mannered guy, he was the one to make sure we made it through the divorce as something akin to friends, for our son's sake.

"Yep." I stand and face him, my hand on Troy's shoulders because I can't let go of him.

"That's such great news." I can tell from his smile that he's genuinely happy for me.

Troy shows his excitement by leaning against me. He barely asks after Leigh these days. He's too preoccupied with starting High School and balancing on the edge of puberty.

And it is great news. And Gerald is Troy's dad and still a good friend. We've successfully co-parented our son for almost seven years now, so why not tell him first? For a fraction of a second, it takes me back to when I found out I was pregnant with Troy. I was only twenty-five. Barely out of college. We'd only been married a few months. This pregnancy couldn't be more different from my first. The biggest difference will be that there will be no one to rub my feet after a rough day at work, when carrying a baby may weigh on me, and have me sink into the sofa with pure exhaustion. If something were to go wrong, or I need emergency help, I'll need to actually think about who to call first, as opposed to having the automatic reaction of calling a husband or partner.

"Anything you need, Jodie. This guy and I will be there for you. Right, buddy?" He holds up his hand for Troy to high-five. Troy slaps his palm against it, and I do feel a twinge of guilt for robbing my baby of having a father. But he or she will have a big brother. And me. And Gerald in the background. And Muriel and Francine. And Ginny and Susan. And even George on the floor above me. And my parents in Connecticut. We will not be alone.

"Thanks." I nod at Gerald, then turn to Troy. "Ready to go, Troy-toy?"

"Don't call me that, Mom. I'm too old for that sh—" He realizes his error and doesn't pronounce the last word. It's true what they say. Once they're in school they grow up so fast. It doesn't matter that Gerald pays for Hunter College, they learn the same ugly words everywhere.

Most times, I don't even pick him up from Gerald's anymore. He just walks the few blocks that separate his father's home from mine. He'll be going off to college before I know it.

"Let's go," Troy says and reaches for his bag. He's not too old to let his dad kiss him on the cheek and give him a big hug. Thank goodness.

"See you next week," Gerald calls after us.

Troy is silent on the way home, but I can tell a million questions are flitting through his mind. I explained the process to him as best I could, going into details where it was appropriate but leaving out the information that no young teenage boy needs to know about his mother.

"So we'll never know who the dad is?" he asks again when we've almost reached our building. "Not even my sister or brother will know?"

"I chose an anonymous donor." I remember going through the details of the men who had donated their sperm. The donor files only consisted of a list of characteristics like height and hair color, medical history, and level of education. At first, instinctively, I sought out tall, blond lawyers until I realized I didn't need that sort of reminder for the rest of my life. "We only know a few things about him." Troy already knows this, but perhaps learning the news while at his dad's has triggered some new emotions in him that need to be processed.

"Mm." He just shrugs and reaches for the key in his pocket. I take him by the shoulders and make him face me.

"Any questions you have. Ask them, please. Okay?"

"Yeah." He pushes his hair away from his forehead awkwardly. "What are we going to call… him or her?"

The fact that he says 'we' makes my heart sing. "Any ideas?" I ask, although I already have plenty of my own. He opens the door and we walk up the stairs in silence, while he ponders.

"How about Rufus for a boy?" he asks.

Personally, I was thinking more along the lines of Jack or Tommy, but I don't want to dash his hopes. "Maybe." He's already half-way to his room. "Why don't you make a list? Give it to me in a few days?"

He nods pensively. Pushes his hair away again, then shoots me that grin. "I'm very happy for you… for us, Mom." And my heart is in my throat.

"Thank you, baby." I lean against a hallway cabinet with my hip. "Are you up for all the extra chores that come with being the child of a pregnant woman?" I shoot him a smirk.

"I've got homework." He takes a few hesitant steps toward his room.

"And you'll have to learn how to change diapers. You'll make the perfect husband for someone some day, baby," I joke.

I never meant for the age difference between my two children to be so big, but what with Leigh coming along and diverting me from the path I had laid out for myself for such a long time, this is how it's going to be. Troy will be even more of a teenager by the time this baby joins us. I've worked with enough moody, irresponsible, hormonally imbalanced teenagers to know exactly what they can be like—and that it's foolish to hold most of their mistakes against them, unless they break the law. It will be an interesting combination. And Troy is not just any teenager. He's my son.

"Come on, Mom." I can see a flush rise up his neck. It's the Irish in him. "Lay off."

"Go do your homework. But stay off the internet." I smile as he exits my field of vision, and then, as it does so many times, my eye wanders to the one picture I kept of her. The only one on display. It's only hanging on that wall because Troy insisted. Because every time I took it down he would stare at the empty spot with a trembling lip. Now, I can barely remember the last time I saw him cast a glance at it.

It's a snap of Leigh and Troy and a giant Lego castle. That's what they did most together. Build things. I never had much patience to sit on the floor with Troy and help him, but Leigh loved it. She could spend hours studying the instructions, laying out the pieces, and making Troy feel like he'd been the one who'd put it all together, with just a tiny bit of help from her.

He beams with pride in the picture, and Leigh's smile is so wide, so genuine, you would never have pegged her for a woman with no desire whatsoever to become a mother. I know she loved him. But she left, anyway. Now I have another on the way. I put my hand on my belly. I'm not really showing yet, but just putting my hand there makes it more real. And then that sneaky feeling, that if she were here, that if she'd stayed and could put her hand on my belly, she would have felt it, too.

Six months later Rosie is born, and my life becomes a whirlwind of not enough sleep, breastfeeding, never-ending noise, folding baby clothes, and never having enough energy to start a new day, but always doing so anyway, and enjoying every minute of it.

A few months after bringing Rosie home, I find myself standing in front of the picture of Leigh and Troy, Rosie in my arms, introducing her to Leigh.

"This pretty woman next to your brother," I say, "is Leigh Sterling." And I'm not overwhelmed anymore by a sense of loss, or missing out on another life, because I know that I've become what was in my cards all along: a mother, again.

"She was a bit crazy, this woman," I say to Rosie. "She didn't want an adorable, cute, awesome baby like you, Rosie. Can you believe that?" And I can smile now because the hurt has been replaced by so many other emotions. "She must have been crazy for not wanting that, huh?" I inhale my daughter's scent while staring at Leigh. I pondered sending her a birth announcement card, but it felt like rubbing it in too much. Like exclaiming, *look how happy I am without you*, and that didn't feel right. Because I could never in my right mind claim that Leigh leaving had made me even remotely happy.

Thus, I haven't seen Leigh since she came to pick up the last of her boxes, months overdue. Last I heard she moved to San Francisco. I bet she's a hot-shot lawyer there. I bet she gets all the girls. I bet our lives are now so completely different we couldn't even be friends if we tried.

CHAPTER SEVEN

Another weekend, another woman, I think, as I let Karen into my apartment. It's my third rental place in San Francisco. After I first arrived, I lived in the financial district to be close to work, but it was too dead and lonely after dark. Then I moved south of Castro, but that brought too much temptation for one more martini after I'd had three already. Too close to Cherries to not pop in and see who would give me the time of day.

Now, I'm on Lexington Street in the Mission District and I've sworn it will be my last rental before I buy a house. If I keep working the way I do, the road to making partner is wide open. My very own house will be the reward for the life I chose when I left New York.

I don't tell all this to Karen. Karen is not here for a chat. We both know what she's here for. She may as well be called Lynn, like the woman I brought here last week, or Fran, like the one from a few weeks back.

"You're playing the field, huh," Sonja said when she came to visit a month ago. "Good for you." Only, it didn't feel good. It doesn't feel good now, either. Yet, I can't seem to stop myself.

What felt good at the time Sonja said it, though, was seeing *her*, someone from what I now consider 'my old life'. San Francisco has given me everything I thought I wanted, and my life is not an unhappy one—from what I hear from tipsy colleagues and acquaintances in bars it might even be an enviable one—but let's just say it doesn't feel exactly how I had expected it to.

Take this woman who is sitting on my sofa while I fix us another drink. She's petite, with slicked-back dark hair, and her eyes sparkle when she looks at me, as if she knows what she's in for—maybe I've built a reputation for myself in more than one field? Even this sort of formulaic foreplay doesn't satisfy me anymore. And it used to be such a thrill. Sitting at the bar at Cherries. Occupying my favorite spot in the corner, the one with the best view. A shot of whiskey at hand. Scoping out the place. Sometimes, I don't even have to try. They just walk up to me, as Karen did earlier. Because I knew what I was there for, I didn't fend off her barely concealed advances. And every time I meet someone, there's this twinge of hope, like a feebly flickering flame that gets a fresh rush of oxygen, that this time it might be different. That I won't know if I don't try. And then I try. And run out of oxygen after one night.

Maybe it will be different with Karen. I have to believe that, which is why I repeat this cycle of hello-goodbye over and over again. This is San Francisco. The number of happy lesbian couples must be higher here than anywhere else in the country —except, perhaps, for Portland. I see them everywhere. Doing groceries together at Whole Foods. Strolling through Dolores Park hand in hand. Every time I go to the movies, one of my favorite means of escape, a *Happy Lesbian Couple* is seated in the row in front of me. As if destiny is trying to tell me something. I haven't figured out if it's that I could be part of a couple like that as well, or that I was a fool to destroy the one I was part of in New York.

"Cheers," I say, as I hand Karen her martini.

"What a lovely place you've got." The wrong remark. After moving three times in the course of two years, my decorating touch has become lazy instead of sharp. I just don't bother with hanging up picture frames or having the right color of curtains made anymore. Why would I if I know I'm just passing through?

"Thanks," I say, anyway. I can hardly dismiss her because she's trying to make polite conversation. There's also something about her that draws me to her more than to others who have sat on that couch. Maybe it's the tint of her irises. They have green flecks in them. A rarity I've always found highly attractive.

We've already covered the what-do-you-do and where-are-you-from bits of our biography at the bar. The preliminary work has been done. All I need to do is swoop in—because God forbid someone swoops in on me. The closest I can get to allowing someone to make the first move is having them walk up to me while I'm nursing a drink, my demeanor an open invitation. After that, it needs to come from me. I determine the pace. Decide where we go—always my place. And with me on top.

"Have you lived here long?" It's this small talk I can't stand.

"Long enough," I say, and move in. I take her glass and deposit it on my designer coffee table. I take her now free hand in mine and examine it, giving the impression I can read her palm. Run my thumb over a line. Press a little. Her lips part already. Then I drop her hand and bring mine to her jaw, cup it briefly, before rubbing my thumb along her lips, demanding entrance. Perhaps it would have been politer to kiss her first, but I need to gauge the sort of woman I'm dealing with. This is how. If she protests too much it's probably not going to work out.

Karen sucks my thumb between her lips with the kind of gusto that never fails to turn me on. This night may not be a total loss, after all. There's promise in the way she twirls her tongue around my thumb, and in the way her green-speckled eyes find mine. Okay then.

I grin at her as I remove my thumb from between her lips. The main issue with a string of one-night stands is that the first time can touch the edges of what I really want to do, but it can never go any further. The irony of what my love life has consisted of these past few years is not lost on me. Always searching, never finding. At first, I was just looking for the next Jodie, until it dawned on me that that was hardly fair on anyone.

Karen lets her head fall back, exposing her neck to me. Is she not the kissing kind? We'll see about that.

"Get up," I say and lead by example. "Come here."

Before she stands, she peers at me from under her lashes for a few seconds, as if she wants me to make her. Then she rises, and I pull her toward me, hoist her top over her head in the same movement. No bra. Just a pair of leather pants and the sort of high-heels I only wear in court when I have something impossible to prove. I do like what I see. I feel it twitch in my muscles, and between my legs.

I walk us toward the nearest wall and push her against it. I curl my fingers around her wrists and bring them above her head. Her breasts jut out and the desire to take her nipple into my mouth overwhelms me. But I resist. Instead, I unbutton her trousers and lower her zipper.

"Keep your hands above your head," I murmur before taking a step back and taking in the view. She looks so vulnerable and defiant at the same time. Her skin is pale against the black of the leather, her lips smudged red. This is a test for me as well. I wish it didn't have to be. I wish I could just enjoy these few hours we have together. Give her what she wants while tending to my own needs. A perfect transaction of fulfilling emotional and physical needs. But sex is rarely so uncomplicated.

Then I give in. Take a step toward her and kiss her fully on the mouth, my tongue meeting hers in a soft crash of desire and lust and trying to make up for too much accumulated disappointment. But maybe I *am* ready. The thought shocks me at first. But why wouldn't I be? I've relocated. My career's on track. I know Karen doesn't have any children. The first thing I will have to ask her about in the morning is where she sees herself in five years.

I pinch her nipple hard and she barely even shudders. Her lack of obvious response turns me on. I pinch harder and she writhes a tiny bit against me and it reminds me that all I really want is someone who can take it the way Jodie did. To meet my match in this game of give-and-receive.

When we break from the kiss, my fingers still on her nipple, she stares into my eyes and flits her tongue over her lips. "Harder," she says, and it's as if someone has flicked a switch in my brain.

———

The following morning, the light wakes me, pouring in through the flimsy curtains that came with the apartment. Before I open my eyes fully, I align my memories of the night before. The bar. The walk over here. A woman named Karen who got to me. Three hours of sleep at most because I couldn't get enough of her, and she kept asking for more, harder, wider. Already, my lips are breaking into a smile. I open my eyes to slits. Karen is so tiny, she's barely a presence in my bed. She's moved to the edge, her body curled into a ball, her head next to the pillow.

I crawl toward her, spoon her small frame with my tall one. We fit snugly together. That's a start.

"Morning," I whisper in her ear. I revel in the absence of regret.

She turns on her back, my arm sliding onto her bare chest. My bedroom smells of sex, of good times had. "Hey." She smiles up at me. Her lipstick is smudged all the way around her mouth and her mascara has left black marks on her cheeks.

There's no awkwardness, no anticipation for a hurried walk of shame out of my apartment.

"Coffee?" I ask. If we drank too much alcohol last night, we sweated it out in bed after. I feel no signs of a hangover, only an already returning pulse between my legs. My eyes wander to the scarf with which I tied her wrists to the bed and I feel all fuzzy inside.

"Sure." Her voice is a bit hoarse. "But something else first." She pulls me toward her and kisses me. It's deep from the beginning and I get lost in it so much I don't realize she's pushed herself up and is now half on top of me. She kisses my cheek next, then my chin, and moves down with more incremental pit stops, and by the time she's reached my belly button, I spread my legs easily for her. I want her there. And when she licks me, I don't think of anyone else. My mind just goes blank while my body surrenders. And I know it's the beginning of something.

CHAPTER EIGHT

"You need to get laid, girl," Muriel says. "How long has it been?"

She says the exact same thing to me every Friday after work. This time, I try to humor her with a truthful reply, but the truth is that I can't even remember. "I honestly don't know." The last time I had sex was with Leigh, that I do remember. First I was grieving. Then I had Rosie. It's Rosie's first birthday next week. So, I guess I could actually count the months—years—since that time Leigh came to pick up some of her stuff, but the prospect is too depressing.

"All jokes aside." Muriel's face goes all serious. "You need affection, honey." To prove her point she puts her hand on my arm.

I stare at it as though she's making a move on me. "Oh, hell no." She doesn't remove her hand, however, just squeezes a bit harder. "Francine won't be having any of that." She cocks her head. "Besides, it would only put our excellent working relationship in peril."

I swat away Muriel's hand. "I've got you. I've got my children. I've got my job. My friends. I don't need anything more."

"Keep telling yourself that until you believe it, sweet pea." Muriel drinks from her mai tai.

"Maybe you're right." I don't usually concur so easily. "But I come with a lot of baggage."

"Everyone does at our age." Muriel shrugs. "Does this mean I can finally set you up with Amy?"

Amy Bernard. I've heard so much about the woman from Muriel I feel as if I already know her, although we've never met. I even googled her, just out of curiosity.

"We'll babysit. You'll have nothing to worry about."

"Nothing to worry about? How about selling myself to another woman with my stretch marks and scars and two children?"

"Amy has children." Another fact I already knew. It's supposed to reassure me, but it doesn't. I can't stop thinking about all the possible complications. But I also know I need to start somewhere. A woman hand-picked by my best friend can't be that bad a starting point.

"Fine. Set it up."

Muriel takes a deep breath, as if she's just been bequeathed with the most important task of her life. "I won't let you down, Jodie. I promise."

Much to Muriel's delight, Amy and I click. I've *gotten laid* several times, and it has certainly taken an edge off, but when I say 'harder' to Amy she can't interpret it in the same way that Leigh used to. Instead, she narrows her eyes and looks at me with a tad too much disbelief displayed on her face. She tries, I know that, just as I know that it's not really a matter of trying.

But I'm not the same woman that I was with Leigh. My relationship with Amy is based on entirely different pillars than supreme and, at times, shocking satisfaction in the bedroom. Amy has two teenagers who are around Troy's age. Two boys. When we're all together I sometimes look at Rosie's crib in fright, what with so much unbridled youth running around the house. Troy is fiercely protective of Rosie, and sometimes it feels a bit like an us-versus-them situation, but then I'm reminded of the solace and comfort I've found with Amy, and more than anything, the deep understanding of each other's lives that we share.

I don't question Amy when she cancels a date because one of the boys is unwell. I don't wake her up for a bout of uninterrupted sex on the rare Sunday morning when we can both sleep in and have either her house or my apartment to ourselves. I don't have to ask her what her week will look like because my week looks about the same.

"I knew you needed more than to get laid, Jodie," Muriel tends to say. "That was just my hook, you see?"

It's only over brunch to celebrate our one-year anniversary, when the conversation turns to moving in together, that I experience the first major doubts. Being with Amy is the complete opposite of being with Leigh. Amy and I never had the urgency of desire I had with Leigh, but the sexual component of our affair has gone from taking a back-seat to a tired, almost reluctant show we put on every few weeks just because it's part of the relationship deal. We've never sizzled in the bedroom, but a spark now and then would be welcome.

Amy has a big house in Park Slope—an inheritance from her late father's side of the family. One that would fit me, Troy, and Rosie easily, but just the notion of leaving my apartment and my neighborhood makes me queasy—not a pleasant sensation when having brunch.

"Think about it, Jodie." Amy has a million freckles on her face and a huge mane of red curly hair. "Rosie could have her own room." Rosie's room at the moment is a glorified broom closet, and the fact of the matter is that on my salary I can't afford to leave my rent-controlled apartment. As far as persuasive arguments go, Amy has come out with the big one from the start.

"I'll think about it."

"Don't sound so enthusiastic." Amy's eyes dim. Sweet, sweet Amy.

"It's only been a year, though." What if it doesn't work out, I add in my head, and I will have lost my apartment.

"Yes, but what a year it has been." Amy reminds me of the reason why we're drinking champagne today. She raises her glass. "I love you, Jodie."

Amy didn't have any issues with the fact that her boys are practically grown and I brought an infant into the mix. The way she is with Rosie, treating her like one of her own, warms me to my very core. In front of me sits a woman with the same desires as mine. The sort of woman I wanted all along. Someone to share my life with—the kind of life I always dreamed of. So what's stopping me? I drink from my glass, which I still hold in toast position.

"Okay." I nod, more to convince myself than her. "Let's do it." In the back of my brain, I can't help but conjure up possible scenarios to keep my apartment. As though a little part of me already knows this relationship—shacked up or not—can never last.

Amy beams me a smile. She is gorgeous. I should have taken Muriel up on her offer to matchmake much earlier. Even Gerald likes her. Most of the time, Troy loves that he's gotten two stepbrothers out of this. Sometimes, though, he just wants to be alone. He grew up an only child for the longest time. "Let's have another." She points at the near-empty bottle in the ice bucket. "Make this a proper celebration."

We planned this day like it would be a wild one. Luxurious brunching followed by luxurious fucking. The boys have been carted off to their dads and Rosie is with Muriel. But I know exactly how this will end. Stomachs too bloated from too much food and booze. Libidos remaining dormant because, in my case, what's the point, really? I'm not sure how Amy feels about our lack of fireworks in the bedroom. Maybe I should ask her. She's sufficiently tipsy to give me a straight answer.

"Are you sure?" I lean over the table. "We could also get out of here semi-sober and, you know, go home."

"*Our* home." She quirks up her eyebrows suggestively and extends her arm over the table. "I'm so happy."

"Me too, babe." I grab her hand. "So, what do you say?"

She glares at me for a minute with glazed-over eyes. Amy is no fool, of course. Not even with a good amount of alcohol in her blood. But, suddenly, I feel we need to have this conversation now. If we don't, there will always be something more important keeping us from having it. This is *our* day alone.

"I say that you look like a woman who has something on her mind." Amy's voice sounds skittish.

I look at our intertwined fingers instead of at her face. My cheeks grow hot already. Leigh and I never had to have these sorts of discussions. It was all so effortless and easy. Then again, Leigh proved allergic to my wish for another child, so what is more important to me? Amy, who wants to lead the life that I want? Or someone like Leigh, who thrills me in the bedroom but can't stick around for the hard stuff? The stuff life is actually made up of. Ideally, I'd find a combination of both in one person, but that's proven to be impossible—as though the two lifestyles are mutually exclusive. Except for me, I think.

What I really want to say is, "I want us to go home and fuck," but I can't use that line on Amy. It's not who we are.

"Sweetie?" Amy urges. I've probably been silent for too long. "Are you okay?" Sometimes, without her being able to help it—and I know this because this happens to me as well—she uses her baby-addressing voice with me. It makes me feel like the most unsexy creature that ever walked the earth.

"I'm fine." I straighten my spine and wave her off. "It's nothing." My liquid courage evaporates. What am I doing anyway? I should thank my stars for having Amy in my life. Or, as Muriel puts it, shower my best friend with eternal displays of gratitude. Normally, I would discuss the lack of bedroom action with Muriel, but she introduced me to Amy, and it seems ungrateful. The fact is I don't have anyone to talk to about this. Perhaps if Leigh had stayed in New York and we'd found some way to become friends. Perhaps we could have discussed this sort of thing. Or would it have led us somewhere dangerous? Either way, there's no point in contemplating this. Leigh Sterling is long gone, and probably rocking another woman's world on the other coast.

Then Amy surprises me. "Come on. We're getting out of here." She signals the waiter for the check. Has she been reading my mind?

"Tell me what you couldn't say at the restaurant," she asks when we're in the cab. The Brooklyn Bridge looms in the distance. I don't even particularly like Brooklyn with all its hipsters and gentrification, I think for the umpteenth time.

I pull her toward me until her ear is close enough to my mouth. "I want us to fuck," I whisper. I put my hand on her upper thigh and dig my fingers in hard. The thing about making demands like this is that it doesn't really suit me. It makes me sound like someone I'm decidedly not.

"Then that's what we'll do," Amy replies, but there's a sort of resignation in her voice I find hard to bear. Like it's a chore that needs to be ticked off a list. "Let's just behave for a little while longer for the cabbie's sake." She glances at the front seat nervously and puts her hand on mine, detaching my fingertips from her jeans.

The rest of the ride passes in a tense silence. While Amy searches her purse for her keys I look over the facade of the house, all three floors of it. There's a basement playroom for the boys, and a woman comes in twice a week to clean it. Rosie could have a well-lit space of her own with room for all her toys, and a desk when she gets older, and real privacy. Maybe I have to do this for my children.

So, I remain silent when we go inside, dump our overcoats and bags in a specially designed closet, and fall onto the sofa, both of us lazy and heavy-limbed. Amy flicks on the TV and there's an episode of *Law & Order: SVU* on and we both love that show, so we watch it and the day passes quietly. Almost politely.

When we go to bed, I'm painfully aware that we have the house to ourselves, like a ticking clock reminding me that it's now or never. Come tomorrow, Rosie will be back, and the boys will arrive in the evening, and our attention will be divided among them, with only a fraction left to spend on ourselves and each other. Then Monday will roll around, and along with it the frenzy of a working week, during which we usually fall into bed completely exhausted at ten.

I'm more put off by my own ambivalence than anything else. I'm fully aware that our lack of a sex life is as much down to me as it is to her. Perhaps even more. Sometimes, when I want to instigate lovemaking, I stop myself because I know I won't get out of it what I really want—hands tied to the bed and five fingers inside. What aggravates me most is that, before Leigh, this more gentle lovemaking would have been more than plenty. Happiness would have been a given. If only Leigh hadn't looked into my soul and given me what I truly wanted.

"Good night, babe," I say to Amy. I kiss her on the cheek and there's a brief moment during which the chaste kisses we exchange may turn into a full-blown French kissing session, but the moment passes, as do so many, and a few seconds later the lights are off and we've both turned on our side.

CHAPTER NINE

"Tell me about your ex," Karen says. We've gone for a walk in Dolores Park and it feels right, for the first time since I arrived in San Francisco, to hold another woman's hand in mine. For the first time, the presence of other couples around us isn't a brutal reminder of how lonely my life has become since I moved here.

"Which one?" We both know it's a lame joke. I've only ever talked about Jodie.

She leans her weight onto me. "Come on."

Karen has turned out to be quite the foul-mouthed little spitfire in the bedroom, always asking for more, making demands, because she knows what the consequences will be.

"She wanted another child, I didn't." It's how I usually sum it up. It has proven very effective to shut down conversations I don't want to have.

The first time Jodie left me alone with Troy, I was a nervous wreck.

"Can you pick him up from school and watch him for a few

hours, please?" she'd asked over the phone. "I really would like to escort this kid to his new foster parents. I'll be back as soon as I can."

"Sure," I'd said, like it was a logical sequence of events. I guess it was. Jodie and I had been dating for a few months. I'd gone to pick up Troy with her from school and Gerald's house a few times. I knew the drill, so to speak. That didn't mean I had confidence in my own abilities to babysit a seven-year-old. Was I supposed to hold his hand when we walked down the street? Pour him a glass of milk when we arrived at Jodie's? I didn't even have a key.

But Troy, perhaps because he was a child of divorced parents, displayed a great deal of independence—he didn't need me to walk him home from school at all, or so it seemed. Nevertheless, we walked side-by-side, and I queried him about what he'd learned that day. I could just about manage second-grade math with my numbers-challenged brain so I tested him with some sums as we headed to Jodie's place. He solved all of them in no time.

When we reached Jodie's building he produced a key and let us in. Once upstairs, he poured his own milk and started playing with an early-model cell phone Gerald had given him.

"I'm texting my dad," he said. "I would text Mom as well, but she doesn't have a cell phone."

I didn't even have a cell phone back then, but I quickly added it to my list of objects to acquire as soon as I quit my ADA job and found a law firm to join. If Gerald had one, I wanted one too.

"Can you show me?" I asked, and took a few steps in his direction.

"Sure. Look." The screen was tiny and so were the buttons he pushed, but it seemed easy with his agile child's fingers. "I'm texting Jake. He's had one for ages."

I'd heard Jake's name mentioned in conversations between

Troy and Jodie. The pupils at the private school Gerald paid for all had cell phones.

I watched Troy's little fingers push the keys in quick tempo until he stopped to show me what he'd typed, before pressing a button with a green telephone on it to send.

"It's so cool," Troy said.

The D.A.'s office had only acquired its first personal computer a few years earlier. It was only a matter of time before Gerald bought one for Troy—perhaps he'd already done so and Troy had one in his giant room at his father's house, despite Jodie's opposition. She'd only agreed to the cell phone because it made her feel safer to know that Troy could reach her and Gerald at all times. Jodie and I had only been dating a few months and I stayed well out of her and Gerald's parental disagreements. Troy already had two parents, and I doubted he needed a third.

After that first time, I started picking up Troy from school at least once a week—saving Jodie quite a bit in babysitter fees. Some days, I would have work to finish and I'd sit at Jodie's dining table while he continued building something elaborate in Lego. Other days, I'd join him on the floor, my long legs often an obstacle, and the hours until Jodie arrived home would pass as if they were minutes.

But, throughout the time we spent together, I was always aware that I was not an extra parent to Troy. He already had a mother and a father. As we grew closer, I saw myself as more of an aunt-like figure in his life. I didn't need to be anything else to him.

When Jodie started talking about having another child, it unsettled me because this boy or girl would be ours. There would be no Gerald living around the corner. No other name on the birth certificate. I would be a mother—a thought that scared me so much it cost me everything.

"I just don't have it in my DNA, Jodie," I said to her. "The maternal gene does not exist within me."

"That's so not true," she said. "What about Troy? You are so great with him."

"It's not the same." I never knew how to explain it adequately to Jodie without hurting her feelings.

"Why not?" she insisted. "What would be so different?"

"Everything." There wasn't a thing between us that wouldn't change if Jodie had another child—and that's how I always saw it: Jodie having another child as opposed to the two of us as a couple going through all the steps to conceive of one.

"Only in the most exhilarating way," Jodie said.

"I've just joined a top firm, Jodie. I can't just hop out of the office and pick someone up from daycare or school anymore." Did she really think that I'd paid my dues at the D.A.'s office, working for a pittance for years, to throw all that hard work away and dedicate my life to another human being for the next eighteen years?

"As I can tell you from experience, working a full-time job and being a mother are not mutually exclusive. I can call millions of additional witnesses to the stand if needed. Yes, life will change. Things will be crazy for a while, but there's no unwritten law of the universe that says you can't have both, Leigh."

How was I supposed to tell this woman I loved so deeply that I didn't want both? That before I met her, the thought of becoming a mother had barely crossed my mind? That her, me, and Troy was more than enough for me? That I was so selfish as to sometimes curse Gerald when he asked if we could take Troy for a night during his week? That Jodie co-parenting a son was about as much as I could take, no matter how much I cared for him?

I never did tell her these things. Not until it was too late.

. . .

"You don't want to talk about her?" Karen caresses my hand with her thumb.

"There's not much to say." I could probably fill a thousand pages detailing my sentiments regarding Jodie—how meeting her changed my life—but I'm not the sharing kind. And it feels as if my wounds have only just begun to heal.

"It's not good to keep it all inside."

"Why do you want to know?" If Karen is going to go all shrink-like on me, I need to go on the defense.

"Because... I feel as if I'm competing with a ghost from your past."

"It's not a competition." I unlace my fingers from hers and wrap an arm around her shoulders instead.

"It sure does feel like one at times," Karen says.

Karen and I have only been seeing each other a few weeks. What is she expecting? "Really?"

"You're so guarded, Leigh. I'm just trying to find a way in." She puts her head on my shoulder. "I like you, that's all."

"That's all, huh?" I stop walking and face her, cracking a smile. "I like you too." I pull her close for a kiss, and while I shut my eyes, inwardly I scream. *Look at me kissing another woman in the park. I can do this. I'm over Jodie Whitehouse.*

But when I kiss Karen it's not the same as when I kissed Jodie. Karen knows too much. She has too much knowledge on how to push my buttons and, even more so, she doesn't need me the way Jodie did.

Jodie and I used to take Troy for walks in Central Park. It was our go-to Sunday afternoon activity on the weekends he was with us. We'd just sit on a bench in silence and watch him play and it's that simple sort of happiness that has eluded me completely since we broke up. As if my life no longer has room for tiny pleasures like that.

On weekends when Troy was with his dad and the weather was nice, I'd take a case file to the park, and I'd read it but never attentively because I could never keep my eyes off Jodie when she was engrossed in a book and she'd suck her bottom lip into her mouth without knowing she was doing it, because she was lost in the story, and she was totally relaxed, and I could almost physically feel the happiness we shared.

She was my soul mate.

When I break from the kiss with Karen I want to answer her question with those words, but that's just not something you say to a person you're courting. I may enjoy inflicting pain in the confines of the bedroom, but I'm not cruel in other aspects of my life.

"Let's sit," Karen says and tugs me toward a bench lining the path. She's so tiny she can pull her feet up onto the bench with her and still sit comfortably. "I guess I'm just trying to understand what made Jodie so special."

She hasn't finished quizzing me just yet. But how can I possibly describe to her that it was everything about Jodie that made her the perfect match for me? Her kindness. Her fighting spirit. Her big, big heart. Her green eyes, and how they could sparkle when I introduced her to a new, unexpected activity after dark. The kind of mother she was to Troy. The way she folded a tea towel just so. How an upturned corner of the living room rug could drive her nearly mad. The softness of her shoulder when she leaned into me after a long day at work, looking for the sort of comfort I was convinced only I could give her. Her long-standing crush on *L.A. Law*'s Amanda Donohue.

I sigh, hopefully indicating that I don't like where this conversation is going.

Karen turns to me, her arms folded around her tucked-in knees. "I don't mean to give you the third degree. I guess I just want to gauge if you're ready for this. I'm not interested in a casual sex partner. I want more, and I think you do, too."

"I do." I nod to emphasize my point.

"Sorry to be so lesbian about it."

"I like the fact that you're such a lez." I cover one of Karen's hands with mine.

"I like many other things about you." Karen slants her head to the right and bats her lashes.

"Come closer." I swat her knees away and she unfolds them so she can shuffle toward me. I grab her by the back of the head and kiss her, so as to stop the thought flitting through the back of my mind: Karen will never be Jodie.

Our lips meet again and again and I focus on the fact that she doesn't need to be Jodie. Nobody else can and will ever be Jodie to me ever again. This is Karen, whom I'm very fond of, and who turns me on, and that, frankly, is much more than anything I've felt since I left New York.

CHAPTER TEN

"What are you thinking?" Amy asks.
Her question jolts me. Have I told her about how Leigh used to ask me that? If I did, I don't remember, but I have been drinking more than I should of late, and sometimes I wake up not remembering exactly what I've said the night before.

"Nothing," I reply. Above us, boys' feet stomp the floor. In a room adjoining the living room, Rosie's sleeping in a bed Amy bought for her especially, so she could nap at her house. The plan is for me and my children to go home after she wakes up. It's what we always do on a Sunday evening. "Just daydreaming."

I wouldn't call this a quiet Sunday afternoon. Amy's had to go upstairs twice to break up a quarrel between her two boys. They seem on edge today, but they're teenagers, so that's nothing out of the ordinary. Troy's been up there with them for a few hours and I presume he's doing all right. Rosie refused to go down for the longest time for her afternoon nap, so Amy played with her until Rosie's stubbornness gave way to extreme fatigue and she as good as fell asleep while maneuvering her toy chicken around the floor.

"You seem troubled," Amy continues. "Is it work?"

I'm glad Amy is not the type of person to ask too many direct questions. She could have inquired about when I'm finally going to take steps to move in with her, but I think we can both do with the peace and quiet of avoiding that dangerously loaded topic right now.

"I could use a longer weekend." I glance at Amy, who's sitting by the window, the light catching in her hair.

"Couldn't we all?" She opens her arms wide. "Come here."

I scoot over to her and lie down, putting my head on her upper thigh. When she starts stroking my hair, running her fingers through it and lightly massaging my scalp, I'm brusquely reminded of how Leigh used to do the exact same thing to me.

Since Amy has asked me to move in with her, and I reluctantly agreed—more in spirit than in action, so far—tension has grown between us. Unspoken, because neither one of us is very keen to address it, but it's there. In unguarded sighs, in phone calls cut short, and in these precious moments of quiet that we have, which we don't want to ruin by discussing our living arrangements.

When Leigh raked her fingers through my hair, whether it happened after sex or not, I felt every caress shoot through me as though it was her love for me itself making physical contact with my skin. The biggest tragedy of Leigh and I breaking up was that, before we couldn't get past our clashing aspirations in life, we hardly ever fought. We had nothing to quarrel about. The ease and pure exhilaration of being with her is what kept me from starting the much-needed discussion about having more children much sooner and in a more serious manner.

When Leigh and I danced around a subject, it didn't feel like it does now with Amy. I happily avoided it because I had Leigh

Sterling by my side. Leigh, who, when I took her to Gerald's house in The Hamptons for the first time, recited a self-written poem for me on the beach. Leigh, who drew our initials in the snow with a stick on the sidewalk outside of our building, and who, I knew, would do anything for me, except the one thing that I wanted so badly.

When I did bring it up in a serious conversation for the first time, I tried very hard to not bombard her with it.

"Troy adores you," I said after she'd put him to bed one night.

"Likewise." She fell onto the sofa right next to me—Leigh would never sit at the other end of a sofa if I was in it. I could listen to her for hours on end about how she believed Troy was so smart for his age, and so incredibly sweet.

"I've always wanted two." My heartbeat picked up speed.

"You've said." For once, Leigh came to lie with her head in *my* lap. She stretched out on her back and stared up at me.

"I'm not getting any younger."

"You *are* getting hotter, however." She smiled and I knew what she was trying to do so I ignored her remark.

"I'm serious, Leigh." I trailed my fingertips through her gel-slicked hair, getting stuck there as well.

"I know you are, sweetie."

I shook my head. "I don't think you do."

"I love Troy to bits."

"I'm not talking about Troy. I'm talking about Troy's potential sister or brother."

"Look, Jodes, if this is a real, burning desire inside of you, we need to address it. But not after nine on a Monday evening. I'm not dismissing you, but give me some time to think about it."

Troy was ten years old by then. I couldn't allow myself to wait any longer, whether Leigh agreed to it or not.

Now, with my head in Amy's lap, when I try to remember

how our civil, quietly spoken conversations turned into full-blown arguments about who exactly was being the most selfish, I fail to pinpoint the exact time. It happened in stages. One discussion ended with a snide remark. The following one was halted abruptly by a few words said in an accusing tone. But, from the very beginning—from that time she lay with her head in my lap looking up at me—I'd been able to sense that we'd never see eye to eye on the subject.

"Are you thinking about *her*?" Amy asks. When feeling insecure, it's easy to give in to paranoia, I conclude, so I don't reply to Amy's question in a harsh tone.

"No, babe. I'm not thinking about anything in particular." Keeping the peace is high on my agenda. I don't want any more fights. I just want to lie here with Amy and enjoy a few more minutes of quiet.

Then, even before I hear it, I see the baby monitor light up green. Rosie's awake. This is how most conversations between Amy and me end. Kudos to her for not making a big deal about that. I count my blessings and get up to fetch my daughter. She'll be hungry now. Amy will feed her—she claims it's important for bonding, and who am I to argue with that?

After Rosie's been changed and fed, I call for Troy. Getting two children and their belongings in a taxi requires my full attention—lest I forget the frog Rosie sleeps with—and my goodbye to Amy is quick and almost methodical.

Sitting in the backseat of a taxi driving away from Amy's house in Brooklyn doesn't sting me nearly as much as it should.

Not the way it stung me when, in the beginning of our relationship, before Leigh had moved in, she would leave my place on Sunday evening to go back to hers, do laundry, and get ready for the work week, and all I wanted the second the door closed behind her, was for her to come back. To break all protocol and just move in, because I already knew that she belonged with me, and nowhere else.

Shortly after Leigh joined Schmidt & Burke, I came down with a massive flu and was bed-ridden for days. Luckily, Troy was at his dad's and he managed to avoid our germ-filled apartment.

I spent the first two days in a fever-induced half-sleep, not very aware of my surroundings. The third day when I ventured out of the bedroom in the middle of the afternoon, I found Leigh hunched over a stack of papers at the dining table.

"What are you doing here?" I asked. It was the first time since falling ill that I'd seen the time and I knew it was only three o'clock in the afternoon.

"What are *you* doing up?" Leigh dropped her pen and scanned my face.

"My back is sore from lying down for the past forty-eight hours."

"Come here." Leigh pushed her chair back. "I'll massage it for you."

"Seriously, Leigh. Why aren't you at work?"

"I'm working from home until you're better." She gestured with her fingers for me to come to her. "Making you chicken soup and all that." Leigh was as far removed from a staying-home soup-making kind of person as I'd ever encountered in my life. "Are you feeling better?" She cocked her head. "I should let Troy know. He'll want to see you. We've both been worried." She reached for the cell phone she'd recently bought. She and Troy were constantly texting back and forth, leaving me entirely out of the loop.

"I think I might be hungry," I said, not expecting her to have actually made any soup. But perhaps she'd gone to the corner store and got a can.

Leigh rose and walked over to me. I was still standing in the same spot. She curved her arms around me, not caring that I'd spent the past two days in bed sweating out a fever. "I called your mother and got her chicken soup recipe. I made the stock from scratch and everything."

"Am I stuck in the most absurd fever dream?" I asked, my head resting on her shoulder. "Who are you and what have you done to Leigh Sterling?"

"I know I don't contribute much to this household in the way of cooking, Jodes, but I step up when I need to." She pulled me closer to her. "I'm so glad you're feeling better."

"I'll have to be sick more often," I joked, but just having my hot cheek pressed against her shoulder was making me feel better by the second.

"Why don't you sit." She started walking me to the couch. "I'll get you a bowl of soup and text Troy. I'm sure Gerald will bring him over after school if he asks."

"Next you'll be telling me you and my ex have become best friends while I was fighting off the flu."

"Very funny," Leigh shouted from the kitchen.

Later, after a few more bowls of chicken soup, which I suspected my mother had made and brought over all the way from Connecticut, Troy arrived and the three of us sat cozily on the sofa, Troy perched against me on my left, and Leigh on my right. Despite not feeling very healthy yet, the combination of starting to convalesce, Leigh's chicken soup, and the fact that she'd worked from home the past three days—her biggest love declaration to date—made a different sort of delirium course through me. The two biggest loves of my life sat by my side while I was ill, when I needed them most, and I wondered if I'd ever been happier, and what could possibly top my sentiments of that moment.

The next day, Leigh left for work, having already stretched her option to not go into the office too far. When she closed the door behind her and left me on my own, I counted every hour until she came home. Throughout the day I felt much worse than I had the evening before when she and Troy had been with me, and it was as though I could, as of that moment, physically assess what love felt like.

CHAPTER ELEVEN

"I never see you," Karen says. "We've been dating for six months but it feels more like six weeks based on the amount of time we've actually spent together."

I'd been so passionate about Karen in the beginning. She couldn't have been more perfect. We shared the same kinky proclivities in the bedroom, and she was free as a bird. No exes hanging around. Fully secure in her lesbian status. No children and no desire to have any. A dentist with a flourishing practice. On paper, it should work.

"We both work too much. I know."

"No, Leigh. I work normal hours. You work insane hours." We're in her apartment in Nob Hill. When I rang the bell half an hour earlier—having knocked off work much sooner than I normally would have on a Tuesday—my head had been filled with the things I was going to do to her. How her pert little mouth would pout, and how the skin of her bottom would color pink under my touch. But she pushed me away as soon as I arrived and sat me down in the sofa for 'a much-needed conversation'.

"I have no choice. You know that. The offer of a partnership could come at any time. I can't start slacking now."

"That's what you have to say?" The side of her mouth twitches a little when she gets angry. I never noticed before. "Well, here's what I have to say." She expels a dramatic sigh. "I don't want to be with someone who rings my bell late at night for a booty call, and is up and gone again before I even open my eyes in the morning. We have no life together, Leigh."

"We have Sundays," I try, because even on weekends I spend many Saturdays catching up on cases in my home office. But I'm the firm's top litigator in San Francisco. I spend a lot of my time in court and juniors and paralegals can't do all my prep work for me.

Karen shakes her head. "You think you're so important."

I'm starting to feel under attack. "This is only temporary. We met at a bad time for me work-wise, that's all."

"Here's the order of importance of things in your life according to me. Work comes first, of course. Then you. And only then do I come into play. You can deny it all you want with your silver tongue and… Bambi eyes. But it won't work. I know what I feel."

I'm a bit taken aback by her accusation that I put myself before her and already arguments start stirring in my brain, but if I turn this into a proper fight, I'm not sure we can bounce back from that. I could take the other route, the only one we've tried and tested successfully. I could back her into a corner—literally—and fuck our problems away. But I doubt that will work with the mood Karen's in.

"You're right," I hear myself say. "I've been a selfish workaholic." I've only become so consumed with work since I moved here. Things were different in New York. Jodie made a lot of accusations toward the end, but she never blamed me for working too much. If anything, she spent too much time after hours worrying about the people she had in her care. "How about we set aside one night a week as a steady date night?" As the words come out of my mouth, I realize I'm signing the death sentence of our very young affair.

"One night a week?" Karen wrings her hands together. "Do you even hear yourself?"

It would be such a pity to lose Karen. I haven't invested enough of myself—and my time—in 'us' to be too heart-broken if it were to end, but she has saved me from doing a lot of things I don't want to do any more. Like bar crawling and one-night stands, and waking up alone on Sunday morning. I decide to fight for her.

"I'm sorry." I slap myself on the chest in dramatic *mea culpa* fashion, only to realize I'm being ridiculous. I don't want to end up hurting her more in the long run. We're very fond of each other, and the fact that she's demanding more of my time can only mean she has strong feelings for me. I also don't want to make any promises I can't keep, because she was right about one thing: my work does come first. I haven't worked my butt off for the past three years to lose sight of the prize now. That would surely make us both miserable, and not be conducive to romantic dinners in Sausalito and picnics with a view of the bridge. "I'm not going to lie, Karen. My work is important. I'm about to make partner, you know that. I have no choice but to put in the hours."

"At what cost, though? Have you asked yourself that?"

I know it's costing me her. Not the biggest price I ever paid. It hurts nonetheless. "If we'd met a year later…" I start.

"Save it. I know your type. Narcissistic to the bone. Think the world stops spinning if you work a few hours less a week. Total disregard for any balance in your life… and for the people who care about you." She chews the inside of her lip for a second. "I'm done, Leigh. When I'm with someone, I want to come first."

This reminds me of one of the perpetually returning arguments Jodie and I engaged in. Her telling me that Troy would always come first. Me replying that I had no trouble with that, that I understood, but what would my place be in the order of importance if she had another child?

"I'm sorry that I can't give you more." I really am.

"Oh, screw it. If you were really sorry, you would do something about it instead of sitting there almost relieved that you'll have even more time to spend on the job now, without someone begging for attention in the wings."

She's right. Every word Karen says is true. I'm out-argued by her precise analysis of our situation. I have no room in my life for love. Not now. At least, I learned a valuable lesson. I won't make the same mistake twice. All my energy will go to the firm from now on. At least until my name is on that letterhead, and for a few years after, of course, to prove that I'm worth it.

"I'll leave." I doubt there'll be room during this adieu for break-up sex. I admonish myself for even thinking that. I rise and head over to Karen.

"You just don't get it, do you?" Karen stares up at me the way she does on morning we do wake up together. As though she just can't get enough. A quality that has drawn me to her again and again—even if I had to resist working overtime once in a while. "Despite you... being you, I'm falling in love with you. Otherwise I wouldn't have bothered having this conversation. I would have just ignored you, and your weekly call, until you forgot about me."

I crouch next to her. Her display of sorrow is really getting to me. If I don't get out of here in the next few minutes, it will be very hard to leave at all. I put my hands on her knees and I can't help it, I feel something spark in my flesh. We have a physical connection between us that's hard to deny. "I have strong feelings for you too, Karen. But as you said... I am who I am." I've hardly felt more pathetic in my life. What happened to the Leigh who would fight for this? Who would at least make a valiant effort and try to make some changes to accommodate a woman who's declaring her love? When did I grow so cold?

"You're making this very hard on me." Karen finds my hands with hers. The skin-on-skin contact blindsides me. I need every ounce of willpower to fight the urge to pull her against me. I'm so torn. I've been in this sort of situation before. Do I ignore who I am and go all out for love? Or stay true to myself and choose the lonely road? If I couldn't change myself for Jodie, how can I possibly expect to be able to do so for Karen? "I'm not asking for the world, Leigh." Her nails dig into the skin of my hands. "If you stop and think for a moment, you'll see that." I look into her eyes. They're shiny with the onset of tears. "I'm not your ex."

Did she really just say that? Instinctively, I want to pull my hands away, but she keeps them chained to her trousers—those leather ones that drive me so insane. "Don't bring Jodie into this. That situation was totally different."

What tethered me to Jodie most was the fact that before me, she was a different person. I changed her, forever. That's a hell of a thing to walk away from. And I wonder how she's doing now. I've heard chatter about a baby girl. Is Jodie happy now? Does she have the life she always wanted? The one I, ultimately, couldn't give her?

"I'm not asking you to co-mother a child with me, Leigh." Karen doesn't back down. "All I want is some more of your time and attention." Her fingers are curled around my wrists. She knows where to apply pressure to make it hurt a little. She knows because I taught her. "We could have a really good thing together. Something you don't just find with any chick who walks into Cherries."

The nights I spent at that bar are still vivid in my memory. Talk about time wasted. The hours I spent drinking away the loneliness, followed by, more often than not, a few hours of disappointment in my apartment—never anyone else's fault but my own. Karen has a point. But she sure is blowing hot and cold, which I understand. She's emotional. Her feelings are on display. I'm not someone who shies away from commitment, and I'm not half the player I believed myself to be when I first arrived in this city. All I want, really, is a steady relationship. Karen knows this.

"What do you want?" I shake my wrists free from her grip easily. "Tell me what you want me to do, and I'll do my very best."

Karen exhales. "I want you to want to leave your office at a decent time in the evening so you can see me. I want you to look forward to that, instead of your next battle in court. I want to mean something to you."

I was expecting more practical instructions, like 'I want you to free up a drawer in your closet for my things'. All I hear now is that she wants promises I can't keep. Then again, I don't want to end up like Steve, my immediate boss in New York, whose wife divorced him two years ago, and who only gets to see his children every other weekend. He may claim he lives for the job, but I've seen his eyes drift to that picture frame on his desk.

"Look, Leigh, I'm not stupid." Karen's voice changes. "I know why you bury yourself in work." During moments of weakness, I may have talked about details of my life I prefer to keep under wraps, such as nagging doubts about the validity of my decision to leave New York. Once I make partner, I could go back if I wanted to. "But, put simply, there's so much more to life than work. I look at people's teeth all day for a living, I should know." The first chuckle of the day. "I didn't mean for this conversation to get so out of hand, I just—just want to make you see. Wake you the fuck up."

"I'm wide awake." I'm still crouched by Karen's side and my thighs are starting to cramp. I push myself up and fall onto the sofa next to her. "You're right, Karen. I shouldn't take you for granted like that. You deserve better."

"Better than Leigh Sterling?" There's a sparkle in her voice. First, she elbows me in the biceps, then, next thing I know, she's straddling me. "I don't think so." Her eyes shine with some sort of newfound confidence. "A better version of you? Oh, yes." With that, she slants her neck and finds my cheek, presses a kiss onto it. "I want you, Leigh. And I know you want me." She's breathing into my ear now, and a plethora of possibilities pops up in my mind. I could fuck her on the couch right here, as a sign of goodwill, but that's not really how we're wired. It would be better to make her wait for it. Make her strip slowly first. And have her stand with her hands against the wall for at least ten minutes, while I watch her backside wiggle in anticipation. I'm not walking out on Karen, and she's not walking out on me.

"I know what you're thinking." Her voice in my ear. "Do it," she hums. And then I do.

CHAPTER TWELVE

In a cruel turn of events, I end up breaking up with Amy in Gerald's beach house. It took years before I was able to return there, and then, when I finally do, hearts are broken all over again. As if the place is cursed. I'm definitely never going back.

It happens three months after we decided to move in together, and I still haven't made any efforts to break my lease, or ordered any boxes to start packing. I made several attempts. I have the letter to my landlord ready on my computer, but somehow I can never bring myself to click the print button. Every time I'm about to, a cold fist clenches around my heart, and a little voice starts yammering inside my head: *Are you sure, Jodie? That's a stupid question, of course. If you were, you would have printed, signed and sent this letter weeks ago.*

My parents have driven down to New York on Thursday and I've introduced them to Amy. The plan is for them to stay throughout the weekend and spend time with their granddaughter while Amy and I take a few days for ourselves in The Hamptons.

It was Gerald who suggested it. "Maybe it will speed up

your decision-making process, Jodie," he had said and dangled the keys in front of me.

And now here we are. Late spring. The smell of barbecued meat in the air and the laughter of children mixing with the voices of their parents. The ocean wild, but perfect for long walks along its shore. Amy looks gorgeous in the twilight dusk, as if her skin tone and hair color were created to shine in this kind of light. And all I can think of is ways to not have this conversation. But there's no way out. It has been brewing for months, its undertones already coming to the fore in the car ride over here, when I was still worrying about Rosie, and checking my cell phone every other minute for a message from my dad. I was certain we'd never make it all the way there or we'd have to turn back entirely before reaching the Southern State Parkway. But my dad never rang, and just before we joined the Sunrise Highway, Amy put a hand on my knee and said, "This will be good for us, sweetie. We need to talk."

"Do you want to go for a walk?" Amy asks after dinner on Saturday. We're sitting on the upstairs deck overlooking the ocean.

"Sure," I say, anticipating how gorgeous she'll look on the beach with her hair untied and her freckles catching the last of the sun. I've practiced some responses to questions she will surely ask, but most of all I just want to know: why can't everything just stay the same? Are we not satisfied the way we are now? Most weekdays I stay in my apartment because it's much closer to work and, honestly—although I would never tell Amy this—during weeks that I have Troy, a house with three teenagers is just too busy for me after a long, hard day at work.

It's different for Amy. She works as an interpreter for the UN, and I'm not saying her job is not stressful, but I'd happily challenge her to do my job for a week and see how she comes out on the other side. After work, she always seems to have boundless reserves of energy to spend on the boys, not that they need much at the age they're at. Scott is sixteen and Ryan fourteen. All they want is to sit in their room or basement and play video games. But it's just their lingering, stomping, boyish presence that gets to me sometimes.

"You're miles away." Amy has hooked her arm in mine. We've taken off our shoes and the water nips at our toes as the waves roll in.

"It's just… this place. I have a lot of memories here. Good and bad."

"Ah… the notorious Leigh Sterling." She pulls me a little closer. "I know you broke up here, but that was ages ago, right?"

And yes it was, even though sometimes, it feels like it was only yesterday that she stood at the front door with her bag in her hand. "Yeah, but I haven't been back since so…" A gust of wind takes us by surprise and sweeps up Amy's hair. I can hardly expect my current girlfriend to feel too much sympathy for my painful memories of ending a faltering relationship with my ex. Amy has had to show a lot of patience with me already, and I'm sure she has limits, too.

"This is the present, babe," she says. "We are here together now. Let's make some new memories."

"You're right. Let's." I lean into her a bit more, and it feels good to be able to do that. To have someone by my side.

"So." She bumps her hip into mine on purpose. "The elephant in the room."

"Is it a pink one?" I joke, stalling.

"It can be, although its color is of lesser importance."

We stop and overlook the ocean. For a city girl like me, it has never lost its power. Leigh used to say that returning to nature is something most people crave on an elemental level.

"How can it not be in our DNA?" she used to ask, when we came here, and stood in a spot like this, arms intertwined. "When we are ourselves nature's finest creation?" She still had the ability to mock herself then, to grin at overbearing things she said. Before things turned sour.

"Is it a sea elephant?" I find myself clinging to Amy's arm, unable to let go.

"Just tell me." Amy's voice has darkened. "Do you ever plan to move in or not?"

I don't say anything for the longest time because I don't know how without hurting her. I can't lie, but she's not going to like the truth either. "I have trouble letting go of my place."

"Why?" She turns to me. "You've lived there for such a long time. Don't you want a change? Live in a more"—I can tell she's searching for the right word—"adult place?"

I could so easily take offense. Tell her that not everyone inherits a house before they turn thirty.

"Or don't you want to live with me?"

I can barely stand her eyes on me. In that very moment, she looks like she already knows the answer. As though coming here is just part of some wishful thinking she has been doing.

"I shouldn't have agreed to move in with you. I wasn't ready." My words sound so cowardly.

"I just find it hard to believe that the reason why you don't want to move in is, and I say this with all due respect to the memories you've made in that place, because of a shoebox apartment which, more often than not, has some problem that needs fixing. Last summer it was the air-conditioning. Last month you had water seeping through the kitchen ceiling. I understand you can be attached to a place, but… don't you want something better for yourself?"

"Tell me honestly, Amy. What's your assessment of our relationship regardless of moving in together or not? Would you categorize it as simply wonderful and great, or lacking in certain areas?"

"For God's sake. Just say what you have to say." Amy raises her voice, not caring about a couple of other beach dwellers walking past us. "Obviously you have an issue with us, so just come out with it."

"Why don't we go back to the house?" I think it better to take the heat off. We haven't wandered far, and I need the time to gather my thoughts.

"Fine." Amy shrugs my arm off her and starts in the direction we came from. She walks so quickly I can barely keep up with her. Already, something inevitable is churning in my gut. No matter the outcome, it's going to hurt.

Back at the house, she heads directly to the fridge and takes out the bottle of Sauvignon Blanc she started at dinner. She holds it up to me wordlessly. Making it seem like too much of an effort to ask me if I want some.

I shake my head. She knows all too well I don't drink white wine. A few minutes later we sit on the sofa, Amy cradling a large glass in her hands, me without any beverage that might lend me some much-needed courage.

"So?" Amy asks. Her tone is milder now.

"I love you," I begin, "and I cherish our life together." Why didn't I say this months ago? "But…" I remember now. Because it's so bloody hard. "We don't have sex, Amy. We might as well be best friends or even roommates in your big house in Brooklyn."

She puffs out some air. "You do know why we don't have sex, do you?" There can't be more accusation in her tone. "Please don't tell me you're so ignorant that you don't have a clue." She shakes her head. I'm not sure if she wants me to reply. Either way, my nerves have turned into a liquid ball of fire in my stomach. All my muscles tense. "From the very beginning…" Her voice is small again. "You made me feel nothing but inadequate. Like what we did was never enough for you. I tried, Jodie. I did my best. And for me, it was enough, but in the end I just preferred not to disappoint you again instead of giving it another go."

Talk about a slap in the face. What strikes me most, though, is that in a year and three months as a couple we've never properly addressed this. "You didn't disappoint me, Amy."

"Oh, please." She drinks from the wine as if it's water. "You want… things… I don't even know what you want. All I know is that I'm not the person to give them… do them to you."

"I'm so, so sorry." I swallow hard. "I certainly never meant to make you feel inadequate."

"Look… what we have now, how things are. That's enough for me. I can live with that. Don't you think we're good together? Good enough to try harder?"

"This isn't about trying harder, Amy. It's about making each other happy."

"Don't I make you happy? You look pretty damn happy to me. There's so much more to life than sex, Jodie. We have our children. Our work. Our friends. Trust me, we wouldn't be the only couple to never do it…"

"But… don't you want to?"

"Yes. Of course, I do. But maybe we're just not compatible that way, even though we make a damn good match in many other departments."

"So, what do you suggest? That we both tone down our desires? That I move in and sleep in a separate bedroom?" I want to run out of the house, toward the ocean, and scream into the roar of the waves. Because, suddenly what I've been missing hits me in the stomach with full force. "Don't you want passion?" I ask.

"This was never about what I want, Jodie. I set my own desires aside for you long ago. And, well, I take care of myself on the many nights that we're not together."

Another slap in the face.

"What do *you* want?" Amy's wine glass is empty and she peers at the bottom. I can't look at her either. There's a reason why we don't have conversations like these.

"I don't want a relationship without sex and passion." Yet, I can't help but think of the implications breaking up with Amy will have on Troy and Rosie's life.

"And that's the real reason why you don't want to move in." Amy's quite matter-of-fact about it now.

"Moving in just seems… like settling for less."

"If I'm 'the less' I can't help but wonder who's 'the more'."

I shake my head frantically. "No, Amy, you're not less. If anything, this is my fault. You did everything right. I just want…" What do I want?

"You want someone like your ex." Amy says it as though she's been thinking about this as well. "I'm not her, Jodie. I never will be."

Maybe I do, but as I sit here and try to imagine my life without Amy in it, it only feels like I want her. "I know," I say, but don't articulate my further thoughts. *You're beautiful, sweet Amy Ballmer, with the red hair, and feet that are always cold, and freckles in places I've never seen them before. You are Amy who sat with Troy for hours until he understood the German verb cases. Who knew what to do when Rosie had colic, when the endless crying was starting to get to me.*

"Either you make the commitment and move in or you don't and… this is over." Amy shuffles nervously in her seat. Where are the tears? The despair? Shouldn't this feel more like a knife through my heart?

"I—I can't move in, Amy. I just can't." I glance at her, expecting to meet anger, but I guess the lack of passion we suffered throughout our relationship is now also manifesting itself during our termination of it—as a blessing in disguise.

"Well then." She looks away again, rubbing her palms on her jeans.

And that's how it ends. With two words of conclusion as nondescript as, perhaps, many characteristics of our life together.

CHAPTER THIRTEEN

"I've given you two months to get your act together, Leigh," Karen says. "Nothing has changed. It's all just words, words, words." She delves into her purse and produces the key I gave her a few weeks ago, as a token of my commitment. "I won't be needing this anymore."

I can't say I didn't see this coming. But the partnership offer came two days after Karen and I had that conversation, and what was I supposed to say? "I'll gladly accept your offer, Mister Schmidt, but I'll need to work less because my girlfriend of only six months needs more attention."

Ironically, because I'm not in my twenties anymore, I'm tired as hell on this particular Friday evening when Karen raises the issue again, because I've just worked a seventy-hour week—of which seventy-five percent are billable hours—and my brain needs emptiness, or alcohol, or something else to unwind. But there's no chance of any of that now.

"I'm sorry." I know I have to let her go this time. It would be too selfish of me to try to keep her. We never made it past the frantic sex stage. Entirely my fault, I know, because more time spent together is required for that. But, honestly, it's not as if I ever felt bone-deep that Karen could be another love of my life. We wouldn't be sitting here again if that were the case. "You're right."

"I knew you wouldn't fight," Karen says. "Last time, I had to encourage you, and yet I was smitten enough to give you another chance. This time, I'm having enough self-respect not to beg." She brushes a tear from her cheek. One that rouses instant regret from my soul. "But I don't want this to be a relief for you. I want you to know, to really know, that this is killing me." She reaches for a handkerchief in her purse. "I hope you feel as shitty as I do now when you wake up alone tomorrow."

I frantically search my vocabulary for words to make this better, to ease the pain, but I come up empty. "You do deserve better."

"Fuck yes, I do." She runs the tissue under her nose. "I'm going." She stands suddenly. I thought she would have more to say, but why would she give me the satisfaction of wasting any more of her time on me.

"Hey." I stand and rush toward her. I can't let her leave as if she were just a stranger stopping by. As soon as I open my arms she falls against my chest, her curled fingers resting above my breast.

"I'm so sorry," I repeat. "You are a wonderful person, Karen. You're kind and funny and... the right amount of kinky." *And I'm sorry I never got to meet any of your friends. And that I had to bail on that party you invited me to last week. And that most of the phone calls I made to you were to cancel our plans.* I don't say these things out loud because they are water under the bridge, and, as she said earlier, "just words, words, words" and when have words ever truly changed anything? "I hope you find someone who does deserve you." Tears sting behind my eyes. Situations like this make me feel like a complete failure. Like I don't have it anymore, the stuff that makes relationships work. Like self-sabotage is all I know.

Karen pushes herself away from me, looks up at me one more time, and heads for the door.

"You're a fucking heartbreaker, Leigh Sterling," she mumbles and leaves. It sounds like the right description of me. I've broken my own heart the most.

After she's gone I pour myself a large measure of vodka. I look around my characterless apartment and decide to give my realtor a call tomorrow. I'm ready for that house now. I've earned it. I need to have at least something to show for—and something to come home to after another twelve-hour day.

My eyes rest on my phone. Out of nowhere, the urge to call Jodie creeps up on me. I glance at the clock. It's 11 p.m. in New York. Would she still have the same number? Does she still live on York Avenue? I still have her mobile and home number stored in my phone. I grab it and scroll to her contact details. My heart beats in my throat. I feel more alive than I have in months, maybe years. Suddenly, the distinct certainty that I have to do this settles within me. That calling my ex at this very moment is what everything in my life after we broke up has led me to.

Because with Jodie there were never any doubts about us making a viable couple. I knew after the first date. I knew weeks before I grabbed her wrists forcefully for the very first time. I couldn't explain to myself why I knew because it was just a feeling, a dizzy spark riding in my veins, making my heart beat faster for her. The way she gesticulated with her hands when she tried to make a point. How she tilted her head when a bout of shyness overcame her. The way she spoke of her job, one of the hardest positions to have in a city like New York, with such zeal, despite the lousy pay and heartbreaking stories that filled her days. I've never seen that kind of fire burn in anyone's eyes as long as I've been alive. Jodie cares. She cares about people everyone else has given up on. And she fights for them. She would rather have gotten fired than have lost a child in the system. But even someone with Jodie's determination and skill to bend the rules couldn't always make that happen. And when rules and the law and the system beat her, she always got back up again. Straightened that spine of hers and moved on to the next case, without ever forgetting about the child that had to be placed in a group home or detention center. Jodie always followed up.

The only time she really cracked was when she'd heard that a boy named Jamal had died. He was barely thirteen years old and already his life had been so unbearable he'd hung himself in a room he shared with three other foster kids. Not even I could cheer Jodie up after that happened. Not for weeks. Yet, she never even for a minute considered changing careers. Jodie never gives up.

I suggested it once, a few months after Jamal's death, after she seemed to have gotten over it for the most part.

"Do you see yourself doing this job until you retire?" I asked. It was our three-year anniversary and we'd gone to The Boathouse to get a good look at the park in autumn colors.

"Don't ask me that." Back then, Jodie hadn't picked up the habit of being snippy with me when I questioned something about her, so I was instantly taken aback. "This job is my life. Who else do these abandoned, abused, uncared for children have in their corner but someone like me?"

I swallowed my follow-up questions—Don't you want to make more money? Have a chance to be promoted? Do something less troubling?—right there and then.

Once she started talking about having another child with the same fire burning in her eyes, I knew I would never be able to persuade her otherwise. If anything, her perfectly articulated reasons to have another made it very clear that I shouldn't even try to stand in the way.

It's 8.05 p.m. My heart is still hammering away. I don't even need to ask myself if she was the one I let get away. I know that she is. Fuck it. I've just been dumped. I'm doing it. I dial her number. It rings. Once. Twice. Then voicemail, but the message I hear is not recorded by her. It's the standard one from her operator.

When she'd first gotten a cell phone, she never switched it off at night. "You never know," she said. I guess that changed when she had another child and sleep became more precious.

I don't leave a message. What would I say? If she'd picked up we could have had a conversation and I could have gauged her reaction, but I don't want to burden her with a message from me on her phone after all these years.

Deflated, I pour myself another vodka. I add a few ice cubes to lessen the sting. I hope the alcohol has the same effect on the sting that comes with being alone all over again. I've made some friends in San Francisco, but they're mainly people from work and more acquaintances than anything else. I don't really have a person I can call when I screw up an affair and who will rush over to my place and get wasted with me. My life might as well be defined by my work. Leigh Sterling, Attorney at Law—nothing else. Full stop.

I raise my glass and mouth 'to dentists' because the world needs good dentists. Although Karen never tended to my teeth in a professional way, I'm sure she's a fine one. And I guess it's only logical that she couldn't talk about her occupation with the same fervor that Jodie did. It's only teeth. I take another sip to stop my mind going down that road.

I let my eyes wander to the cabinet in the corner. I brought some stationery from the office just to be able to look at it. It took a few weeks for the name change—because I was never going to be anything less than a name partner—to trickle through to the office supplies, but it finally did last week. *Schmidt, Burke & Sterling.* It has a much better ring to it than just Schmidt & Burke.

CHAPTER FOURTEEN

After Amy, I have two more affairs that develop into the beginning of a relationship, until I put a stop to them a few months in. Muriel eventually forgave me for breaking up with Amy *for all the wrong reasons* and signed me up to a dating website. Following a few chemistry-less encounters, I found myself in a coffee bar around the corner from my place with a woman named Sheryl. After saying goodbye to Sheryl, I actually had a certain giddiness in my heart and the proverbial spring in my step. She was a foul-mouthed police officer with the most beautiful eyes and something in her demeanor—a certain determination I hadn't come across in a while—that promised fireworks in the bedroom. But, after the initial spark —and subsequent bedroom frenzy—started to make way for more conversation and getting to know each other better, I started to notice that we always ended up at her place and she showed little or no interest in coming to mine or meeting my children.

A single mother with two children is a hard sell and after it became apparent that Sheryl had no real inclination to include my kids in her life, things had to end. I was not going down that road again. But at least I had tried.

After Sheryl, I had a brief fling with the new girl in the legal department at work. Eve was ten years younger than I was, and she reminded me of myself when I was in my twenties. After office hours, we'd just drone on about work some more until it was time to go to bed—because we had to go to work in the morning. Eve was a dainty girl who wore blouses with lace on the collar and shiny knee-length skirts that didn't really do that much for me. After a few months, we decided we'd be better off as friends. I had tried again. Something Muriel was always on my case about. As though she'd decided to promote my relationship status to her most important hobby.

"Life is hard enough already. No need to go it alone," was one of her favorite sayings. I agreed, but for a woman in her early forties, with a body marked by childbirth, and two children to show for it, datable women weren't exactly lining up.

I meet Suzy on the day Troy leaves for college. She appears in the bar where I decide to stop for a drink after having waved goodbye to Troy and Gerald, who is driving him to Berkeley. If it weren't for Rosie, I might have joined them on their road trip, just for old times' sake. As a final farewell to my boy's childhood. And what a fine boy my son has become. He wants to be a lawyer, just like… I'm just about to let my thoughts wander to Leigh when a woman spills half of her drink on my table.

"So sorry." She has as thick a New York accent as I've ever heard. "I'm always a clumsy one. Did I ruin any of your belongings?"

I look from her to the table, which is empty bar a small puddle of what looks like Guinness. I shake my head.

"I'll be right back to mop that up." She flashes me a smile. "Can I leave that here for a second before I cause more wreckage?"

"Sure." She has the kind of smile that lights up a place.

"Hey, Dave," she yells at the barkeep. "I've done it again. Can you throw me a rag?"

Dave rolls his eyes and pitches a cloth in her direction. "You won't catch it," he yells after it. And sure enough, as soon as the rag reaches the proximity of the woman's hands it somehow ends up on the floor instead of between her fingers. She just shrugs and goes to work.

"I'm Suzy," she says to me when my table looks pristine, "Dave's sister. I just moved in upstairs."

I hold out my hand while I introduce myself. "Do you work here?" I ask after our handshake ends.

"Hell no." She tilts her head toward the chair on the other end of my table. "Can I sit?"

"Of course." I'm glad for the company, what with Troy on his way to becoming a proper adult and Rosie spending the day with her grandparents, who've come down to say goodbye to Troy. Our dinner reservation is hours from now. I presumed I'd need some time to put myself together. "Pleasure to have you." Little do I know at that moment that Suzy will almost be enough—almost.

"I start in the bank around the corner next Monday. I just moved back here from New Jersey after the most boring year of my life. I thought I could live outside of this city, but turns out I can't." She drinks from her beer and some of the dark liquid sticks to her lips. Black lipstick would suit her well, I think. She's the type for it. "You can take the girl out of New York and all that…" She narrows her eyes a little. "What's your story? I mean, I do know better than to ask that question to a woman drinking alone in the middle of the afternoon, but if you care to indulge me?" She shoots me a wink. "It beats unpacking."

I tell her about just sending Troy off, and one drink turns into three, and before I know it I have to rush to meet Rosie and my parents at that tacky restaurant they love to go to on Times Square.

"Stop by anytime, Jodie," Suzy says as she leans back in her chair and gives me a very obvious once-over. "You will most likely find me here every night. Dave needs some help making this place more glamorous." She yells the last bit so her brother can hear.

I'm back for more of Suzy a few days later. Just for a quick drink after work. I find her holding court at the bar, regaling a motley crew of bar flies with a story that features a horse and a pig. Her personality is magnetic and I can't seem to get her out of my head. I want to know more. During our conversation a few days earlier she made no mention of having a partner and when she referred to her ex the one time, she didn't call him or her by name. Besides, I know what flirting looks like.

I take a seat at the bar a few stools from her and order a martini from Dave. He not-so-discreetly signals Suzy that I've arrived.

"Excuse me, ladies and gentlemen," Suzy exclaims. "There's a lady here who requires my attention." Her words make me go all fuzzy inside. She kisses me on each cheek and her perfume drifts up my nostrils. Immediately, I regret not having arranged a babysitter. I'll need to leave in forty minutes to pick up Rosie.

"Let's slide into a booth," Suzy says and leads the way. She's dressed in the tightest pair of black jeans I've seen on a woman above forty, a black vest and not much else. Maybe she's making the most of her freedom to dress before she begins work at the bank. When I sit down opposite her, I notice a tattoo of a music note on the inside of her wrist. She's a wild one, I can sense it.

"I was hoping you'd come back." There's that smile again.

Her hair is short but still manages to point to all sides, as if she hasn't owned a comb in years.

"I'm glad I did."

"Any news from your boy?" The fact that she inquires about Troy warms me to my core, just as her mere presence did on the day.

"I only call him once every day," I joke.

When I chuckle, Suzy gives a belly laugh. "How about the little one?" If she wants to seduce me, she's doing an excellent job of it. Appearing genuinely interested in my children really is the best way to go. Maybe I should just ask her out.

"She's at a friend's. I have to pick her up in a bit." I look at my watch. "Sorry I can't stay longer, but, erm, I—"

"Yes." Suzy is nodding vigorously. "Let's go out sometime." She's probably one of the least inhibited people I've ever met. "I would like that very much."

And just like that I have a date with Suzy Henderson, who lives around the corner from my building, whose muscles don't tense when I mention my children, and whose rock-chick exterior and big mouth make my head spin a little.

———

Because of Suzy's extensive knowledge of the bar scene on the Upper East Side we end up going on a modest bar crawl, ending up at Henderson's for a night cap. By the time Dave brings us two whiskeys I'm so hammered I wouldn't hesitate to go upstairs with Suzy if she invited me, although I'd probably end up falling asleep the instant I took my clothes off.

Our first date is pleasant enough, and I get schooled in interesting facts about my neighborhood, but Suzy seems to like a drink, and I find it hard to keep up. Thank goodness it's Friday night and I'll have an entire weekend to recover from this bender.

"God, I'm so tempted to take advantage of you." By the time Suzy says this in her clear, booming voice, I'm not shocked anymore. She peppered our entire evening with forward phrases and come-ons like that. I adore the fact that she has zero qualms about showing interest in me. "But I think, for first dates' sake, it is required that I walk you home and kiss you chastely on the cheek outside your front door instead." She has finished her whiskey already while mine remains untouched.

I chuckle and gesture for her to have it. "I would prefer to remember our first kiss." I look into her blue-grey eyes. They're alive with amusement and joy.

"To our next date, then." She raises her glass and scans my face, her eyes halting at my mouth. "Has anyone ever told you that you have the sexiest lips this side of the Hudson?"

"Oh really?" I curl said lips into a pout. "Who lives on the other side of the Hudson?"

Later, when she walks me home, the heat of the alcohol warms my flesh, but it's also Suzy's presence next to me that heats me up. She's exciting and full of promise and entertaining and, as it turns out, a bit of a lady as well.

As promised, she kisses me gently on each cheek, throws in a stiff, lingering hug—and oh, her body pressed against mine already feels so good—and then leaves. By the time I make it upstairs, my muscles are still tingling and my skin is even more flushed.

I pass by the picture of Leigh and Troy and consider that I haven't felt like this after a first date since the one I went on with Leigh Sterling.

———

My first time with Suzy happens on our third date. Our second one got cut short because Rosie got sick and I received a call from the babysitter a few minutes after I'd sat down at the restaurant. Suzy was such a good sport about it that I was tempted to take her up on her offer to accompany me home and take care of Rosie together, but I guess we both understood that it was more out of politeness that she offered, because a second date was really a bit soon for introducing her to my daughter. Moreover, I wasn't in a hurry to introduce anyone to my children after Amy, because if things didn't work out again it would also be their heart I'd be breaking—and I'd done it to Troy twice already.

For our third date, Suzy invites me to her apartment above the bar for a takeaway and a bottle of wine. We both know what that's code for. By then, I'm so hot for her that in between replying to emails at work, I daydream about kissing the lines of that tattoo on her wrist—much to Muriel's delight.

"Good God, girl," she says, "you're making me miss that exquisite thrill of the first few dates. Have some consideration for a woman who's been faithful to her partner for two decades."

And it *is* thrilling. Knocking on Suzy's door is such a rush, I'm slightly dizzy by the time she opens it. She's wearing tight jeans again, and they make her legs look even longer. She's not a fancy dresser, but I like her casual, no-fuss style. Almost anyone can look good in layers of make-up and the right skirt, but not everyone can pull off jeans and a t-shirt and make it look sexy and inviting.

"Don't mind the mess," she says after she's shown me in. "Dave hasn't bothered to move most of his stuff out yet. Lazy bastard."

"I only have eyes for you," I say.

"Oooh." Suzy brings her hands to her sides. "She flirts." She cocks her head to the side and looks me over. "You're such a posh girl, Jodie." She doesn't say if she thinks that's a good or a bad thing.

The bottle of wine I brought empties quickly, but when Suzy offers to open another I decline. "I don't want to be drunk for what comes next," I say, as I lean back in my chair.

"You're such a lightweight." She says it with a devilish smirk on her lips that ignites something between my legs.

"We'll see about that." I push my chair back and wait for her to come for me.

And she makes me wait, which only intensifies the pulse between my thighs. After a few slow seconds, she walks over and straddles me with her long legs.

"First," she says as she looks down at me, lowering her face toward mine slowly, "we kiss." And then we do. And I've only known one other time in my life that from the very first instant my lips met another woman's, I knew it would be special. I recognize the feeling as it jolts my core and awakens all my senses. With Suzy, it's the real deal. I don't know how I know, or how my brain processes this wishful thinking into actual information, but I feel it course through every cell in my body nonetheless.

Soon, we're tearing off each other's clothes and stumbling toward the sofa in a frenzy of blind, first-time lust. Suzy fucks me while gazing into my eyes, as though she already knows that I like to be watched like that, and I can see her lips curl into a sly grin—another massive turn-on—just before I'm about to come.

And, of course, our first time is not kinky, nor does it push any boundaries. That's not what first times are for. But when we lie in each other's arms afterward, our lips stretching into smiles against each other's skin, I vow not to make the same mistake I made with Amy, and I resolve to openly tell Suzy about my desires sooner rather than later.

CHAPTER FIFTEEN

When I first get the email I blink twice because I think I need to have my glasses adjusted. But there it is: the letters spelling out 'Troy Dunn' the way they've always done, just not in my mailbox. My heart in my throat, I click it open.

Hi Leigh,

I hope you don't mind me emailing you out of the blue—and after all these years. I'm an undergrad at Berkeley now, and the idea is to go to Law School after. I was wondering if you'd like to meet up sometime? Professor Steiger (who teaches Criminal Justice) speaks so highly of you.

I understand if you don't feel up to it, but I'd really like to catch up and pick your brain.

Best,

Troy

P.S. This has nothing to do with Mom. She doesn't know I'm contacting you.

I keep staring at the last sentence. How old is he now? I count on my fingers. He should be in his second year. I don't hesitate and hit the reply button immediately. I may not have a lot of room in my schedule for romantic shenanigans, but for Jodie's son, I'll free up all the time in the world.

Troy was eleven years old the last time I saw him. Saying goodbye to him hit me much harder than I had anticipated, but I could hardly negotiate visiting rights with Jodie because of the reason for our break-up. Plus, I knew it would only make things harder in the long run. A clean break, I thought. From mother and son.

Troy and I met at Jodie's apartment and as a parting gift I'd brought him The Death Star Lego set. He had mostly grown out of playing with Lego by then, but I had bought it for old time's sake. Because it was our thing and I wanted him to have something cool to remember me by.

I saw a tiny spark of excitement flicker in his eyes before they went dim with held back tears. After having to say goodbye to that boy, I swore I would never date a mother with non-adult children ever again, because of the total unfairness of it all. At least that was one goal I set and reached without having to go through a lot of trouble. Since Karen and I broke up, I haven't dated anyone, let alone a mother.

And, of course, in those moments when I looked into Troy's sad face on that rainy Saturday in early May 2003, the question came to me again: *why can't I do this for her? And for him? Am I really that selfish? Am I really putting myself and the pursuit of my career before this boy's happiness?* After all, Jodie had put her desires aside for me. She'd waited until she believed she couldn't anymore, perhaps hoping, in vain, that the passing of time might change my mind. But time passing wouldn't make a mother out of me. Nothing would. Not even six years in the presence of Troy, for whom I cared deeply, but who already had two parents—and I wasn't one of them. I loved him, perhaps as a mother would love her son—I had no way of comparing—but I always believed that if I did, there would never be enough of that to go around for two of Jodie's children. How could I, a person who had zero track record of being interested in mothering children, ever be enough? Or be unafraid enough to try?

"Why are you leaving?" he asked in a small voice I had rarely heard him use.

I exchanged a glance with Jodie and she took over—she let me off the hook again. "It has nothing to do with you, sweetie." She put her hand on his shoulder and squeezed. "I explained it earlier," she said to both of us.

I had prepared some replies to possible questions, the way I did in witness prep but with myself on the stand and an eleven-year-old asking them. There was nothing of the lawyer left in me that afternoon. I wasn't a lawyer, nor a witness. Just a breaker of hearts.

"Can I have one last hug?" I asked, and shuffled a little closer.

I hadn't expected him to throw himself into my arms the way he did, and that floored me most of all. That unspoiled, unfiltered affection.

When I looked at Jodie, her son in my arms, I saw from the look in her eyes that she may one day forgive me for leaving her, but never for doing this to her flesh and blood. I would not forgive myself for a long time either, because to chip away a little at the innocence and, even for a moment, the easy happiness of a child, is not something you recover from quickly.

And now Troy is asking to see me. I reply that I would love to and that he should send me a few possible dates to meet. He responds not long after and a few days later I'm on my way to Berkeley.

He looks more like Gerald than Jodie, but he has her eyes, and that way of hers when he swats away the hair from his forehead with a flick of his wrist. When I extend my hand for him to shake, he pulls me into a hug, and I notice he's taller than me—he must get that from Gerald as well. Overall, he just looks healthy with youth and intense energy. And I have to dig deep to not show all that I'm feeling, have to strengthen my core and straighten my spine and hope that it's enough.

"Look at you," I say, and can't help but shake my head a little.

He shoots me a grin. I'm not sure it contains reflections of Gerald's smile because I didn't encounter that very much. It's not Jodie's, though. Even though it's her son I'm sitting across from, I'm bombarded with memories and nostalgic emotions. But Troy is an entirely different person now. He's all grown up, and I can only imagine how it must have torn Jodie up inside to send him off to college. Did it sting more because he decided to enroll at Berkeley?

"You look great, Leigh," he says. The early spring sunshine produces enough heat for us to sit on the outside terrace of the bar. "I have to admit I was quite nervous about emailing you, but I couldn't not, you know?"

"Yeah." It's way too late for an apology. And Troy seems to have grown into a nice guy, despite me leaving. Even though I know he didn't invite me for a drink to discuss his mother, I have to ask. Before I can say anything else, I need to know.

"How's Jodie doing?" Luckily, I can keep my voice from cracking when I say her name.

"Mom's doing fine." Does she ever visit? I want to ask. Has she been here, in my adopted city? The mere thought sends a shiver up my spine. "And I have a sister now. Rosie. She's six and not at all annoying." That smile again.

Mom's doing fine. What does that mean? Is she with anyone? I can't bring myself to ask.

"She's seeing someone again." Troy answers my question for me. "It seems quite serious. Her name's Suzy. She's good fun."

I nod, hiding my discomfort. "Good to hear everyone's doing well." Unexpected panic floods me. What was I expecting? That Troy contacted me to set me up with his mother again? To hear that things haven't worked for Jodie on the personal front over the years? In the hope she might have let slip that she misses me? *Suzy.* Maybe I can get him to spill her last name so I can google her later.

"How are *you*?" Troy asks. His voice is light and he seems oblivious to the turmoil raging inside of me.

"I get by." A college student who's also the son of my ex is not someone I'm going to confide in.

"Get by, my ass." He slaps the tabletop with his fingertips. "You're the hottest lawyer in the Bay Area." He holds up his hands. "I'm going to be honest with you, Leigh, when I let it drop that I knew you, my status in my Criminal Justice class went right up."

I can't help but chuckle. Meeting Troy isn't about sentimentality. Troy was just a boy when it happened and for him it's all been water under the bridge for years. He's after the clout that comes with being associated with me. I'll happily oblige. "If we need to be seen together somewhere, just let me know," I joke.

I clearly remember the concentration on his face when we made one of these huge puzzles together. He must have been seven or eight, then. His little tongue sticking out from between his lips as he pushed a piece in place, followed by a proud grin.

"I can only take so much advantage of you." He sips from his Coke. "But I could use your help with an assignment."

"Cutting straight to the chase is a good trait for a future lawyer."

"Oh no, not right now. Please don't think that." He blushes. Maybe he does have more of Jodie in him than I caught at first glimpse. "I'm not that slick and harsh just yet."

"We'll work on that too, then." I send him a wicked grin. A short silence falls.

"Look, Leigh…" I can tell he's struggling to say something he's been chewing on for a while. "When you first left, I was angry. Mom explained, but I still didn't understand, you know?" His shoulders relax again. "For the longest time, I was convinced I never wanted to see you again." His lips form a thin stripe in between sentences. "But I grew out of that as well. I understand now why things didn't work out with you and Mom. And I realize it must have been hard for you as well. I mean, you and I were pretty close. So…"

"Thank you for saying that." I swallow the lump in my throat. "Are you going to tell Jodie that we met?"

"I don't know." He shrugs, indicating he hasn't given that particular matter a lot of thought. "Do you think I should?"

"Depends." Just thinking about it awakens nerves I haven't experienced for years. "If we see each other again, you probably should. She'd want to know."

"I guess." His face breaks out into a smile again. "Are *you* seeing anyone?"

"No." I glare at his white t-shirt which strains around his shoulders. At that dark mop of hair that keeps falling into his eyes. There's currently only one heartbreaker sitting at this table. "Not at present."

"Oh," is all he says, because what else can he say? "It was never the same with Mom's other girlfriends, you know."

A flutter in my chest.

"Well, she was single for a very long time after you—"

"I don't know if we should talk about this, Troy." My voice quivers.

"Why? Does it make you uncomfortable?"

"No, but Jodie might not appreciate you telling me about her love life."

"Maybe not, but I can tell you about *my* life, can't I?" Troy Dunn will make an excellent lawyer.

"Of course." Despite what I've just said, curiosity burns inside of me. I want to know everything, even though I'll only end up mulling the information he gives me over and over in my head, trying to draw comparisons, and hoping I still, somehow, in some crazy, illogical parallel universe, come out on top.

"Rosie and I only ever met Amy, and now Suzy. Anyone else she dated never made it past our front door when I was there."

She must have been so careful to keep Troy from being hurt again.

"Amy was all right. She had two sons my age, Scott and Ryan. It was fun to have brothers for a little while, I guess. We almost moved in with them, but then, for some reason, it didn't happen. According to Scott, it was all Mom's fault, but he never really said why."

"That must have been hard." The engine in the back of my brain starts churning. Amy with two sons. "Having other kids around and then having to say goodbye."

"I guess." He shrugs again. "For a while."

"Does Suzy have any children?" I can't help myself. It's like a door has opened, and I need to walk through it.

"No. She has moved in, though." He grins. "She makes such a mess. And you know what Mom is like."

While it was strangely satisfying to hear that Amy and Jodie didn't move in together, it stings that Suzy has made it that far. "Does Jodie still live on York Avenue?"

"Yep. Same old place. I don't think she'll ever leave there. Rosie has my room now, so I usually end up on the sofa when I go home. Or at my dad's."

"That must be rough. To have your room taken over like that."

"If it were anyone else…" He reaches for his phone. "But look at this face. You couldn't stay mad at her for more than five seconds either." He shows me a picture of a curly-haired girl grinning widely. Her green eyes hit me hard. The child in this picture is, put very simply, the reason why Jodie and I broke up.

"She's adorable." I can't hide the agony shooting through me like a freshly sharpened arrow, slicing through my flesh, puncturing everything.

Troy puts his phone on the table and looks at me. "Are you okay?"

But I don't want to fall apart in front of Jodie's other child. The irony of it would be unbearable. "I'm fine."

"Mom eventually told me why you broke up… I mean, I know…" He shuffles in his seat.

My own phone saves me. I didn't bother taking it out of my purse and I have to dig deep for it now, as if I have to linger in this moment of despair as long as possible. "Sorry, it's my boss. I should take this."

Troy nods and starts fiddling with his own device.

I talk to Steve for a few minutes and seize the opportunity to fake an emergency. "I'm very sorry to cut this short, Troy, but something has come up at work. I have to go, but I'd love to see you again." I fish a card out of the side pocket of my purse and hand it to him. "Call me anytime."

"I will." He stands. Does he want to hug again? He just puts his hands on my shoulders and squeezes. "You can be sure of that."

On my way back to the city, I do wonder if I'll ever see him again. Did he see me freak out? I wouldn't blame him for not wanting to deal with that. Rosie's picture flashes before my eyes. Not because I suddenly regret not becoming a mother, but because there were times when I tried to stop Jodie from becoming the mother of that smiling girl.

CHAPTER SIXTEEN

When we drive into San Francisco proper in the a hire car we picked up at the airport, a bout of nerves hits me. But then Rosie yells something from the back seat and I'm pulled into the present again, away from the memories that have crept up on me on this journey.

We've come to spend a few days with Troy in the city. Leigh's city. I thought about getting in touch, because it's been years now, and surely we can be civil to each other, but I have Suzy and Rosie with me, and we're here as a family, and meeting up with exes doesn't really fit into our plans. Also, after all these years, I'm still not sure how I would react to seeing her again.

No, this trip is about family. The one Leigh never wanted. I've never been to San Francisco, but I presume it's a big enough city to not have to worry about inadvertently running into relocated exes. And we don't need a guide because we have Troy.

It's late when we arrive at the hotel. After we've freshened up, had a quick bite and put Rosie to sleep, Suzy and I are huddled on the bed together. I flick through the channels absent-mindedly, until an old episode of *L.A. Law* comes on.

"I love that show," I whisper to Suzy. I don't tell her Leigh and I used to watch re-runs religiously together.

"Oh," Suzy hums. "Hey, was that an episode of *Sons of Anarchy* you just flipped past?"

"I don't know. You want me to go back?" Our arms touch.

"Not if you want to watch this." Suzy moves her arm away from mine. She's trying to say yes by saying no again. It drives me crazy when she does this. She re-adjusts her position so there's a gap between our arms.

"It's fine." I hand her the remote.

"No, you choose." She hands it back.

Ostentatiously, I change the channel.

"You didn't have to do that, babe." She leans into me again and focuses on the men on the screen riding their motorcycles, in which I have zero interest.

I don't know if these minor irritations are normal in relationships. Suzy moved in a few months ago, and I've caught myself suffering from rising levels of aggravation over nothing in particular ever since. They're not fights or arguments that we have, just tiny displays of not seeing entirely eye-to-eye on everything. Not that we have to, but sometimes it gets on my nerves that Suzy can so easily manipulate me into getting her way.

I wouldn't have asked her to move in if I hadn't considered our affair full of potential. I've had to give and take—mostly give when I really wanted to take—but it works well most of the time. When she got fed up with living above her brother's bar, and the noise and nuisance that comes with that, and said she was going apartment hunting, I decided not to make the same mistake twice. And I wouldn't have to leave my apartment if I asked her to move in.

Suzy has been good for me. And her timing was impeccable,

what with Troy having just moved out when we met. Rosie adores her and vice versa. Our sex life is not as adventurous as I would like it to be, but at least we have one. She's easy-going, often messy to an extent that I have to keep myself from dangling a nonchalantly cast-off item of clothing in front of her and ask, "Are you really going to leave this here?" But I know she will just shrug it off, tell me what I want to hear, and do it again the very next day. Some people just don't have neatness programmed into their genes. That, too, I've learned to live with.

We had *the conversation* after we'd had sex a few times. I had tucked my head in Suzy's armpit post-orgasm and lay staring up at her breast, trailing a finger around her nipple.

"You're making me hot again," she whispered, her voice still husky from before.

"That's the idea," I said, decreasing the circumference of the circles my finger drew.

"Oh really?" I felt her shift against me. "What are you going to do to me?"

I pressed a kiss against her side. "I was wondering more what you would do to me." I took her nipple between my fingers and pinched—gently.

"Plenty of naughty things if you keep that up."

I squeezed harder.

"Ouch," she yelped, but there was humor in her voice.

I continued to squeeze.

She pushed herself up and looked down at me. "You're asking for it," she said.

"Yes." Something unclenched between my legs.

"Okay then." The tenderness she kissed me with frustrated me.

"Kiss me harder," I demanded.

She did, but it still wasn't nearly hard enough. I grabbed her by the back of the head and pulled her roughly to me.

When we broke from the kiss, which had been more biting than kissing, she looked at me earnestly. "Why so rough?"

"You think that's rough?" I drew one eyebrow into an arc.

"I don't know if you're aware, but you're always doing this when we make love."

Of course, I was aware. I was doing it for a reason. But I knew I couldn't bombard her with my wishes. I'd learned my lesson from being with Amy. "Yes, I think I'm aware."

"Why don't you tell me what it is you want me to do, so I can stop guessing." There was no annoyance in Suzy's tone, which was a good sign.

"Okay." I sat up a bit. "I like to be dominated. Tied up. Taken." The words came easier than I'd expected they would, perhaps because I'd had many years to practice them in my head.

"You want me to tie you up?" Suzy scrunched her lips together.

"Only if you would be open to that. I don't want to force you."

"I don't know. I guess I would need to think about that. Maybe read up on it." I hadn't anticipated that sort of careful reply from someone I'd come to know as free-spirited and daring.

"Okay." I was starting to feel self-conscious. This was not an easy ask. "I would appreciate that."

No more sex was had that night.

Suzy canceled our next date. She claimed her brother needed help in the bar because one of his staff had bailed on him. "Come by," she said. "But we won't have a lot of private time."

I was paranoid enough to check up on her. If it hadn't been for our conversation a few days earlier, I wouldn't have.

Perhaps I thought I'd find her in a corner of the bar, curled up with some 'literature' instead of bartending a rowdy crowd. But she was indeed pouring drinks and working the customers the way she so easily could.

We were at my place on our next date—a home with many memories.

"Did you have a good read?" I asked, injecting some cheekiness into my voice. I didn't want our upcoming talk to be too heavy in tone. After all, what we were discussing was one of our main sources of fun.

"I did." She regarded me with those glittering eyes of hers. I'd fallen hard and fast for Suzy and I sat there fervently hoping I hadn't put our blossoming relationship on the line because of my question. "Very informative," she teased, and I felt it in my belly.

I sucked my bottom lip into my mouth and waited for her to say something else. Perhaps because I had brought up the subject, I had to be the one to carry the conversation forward, but the nature of it, the coming out as explicitly submissive, prevented me from doing so. I wanted her to know what to say and do instinctively. If that was a mistake on my part, I didn't perceive it as one at the time.

"I can do certain things, but, Jodie, I'm not sure what you think of me, or what kind of person you think I am, but this sort of stuff doesn't come entirely natural to me."

"I understand that." And I also already knew. If it had come natural to her, she would have shoved me against a wall already while delving her fingers under the waistband of my panties, and had me, on her own terms. "I'm just asking if you're willing to try."

"I am." She inched a little closer. "I can tell this is important to you."

I wasn't looking for a second Leigh, nor a second Amy. Just someone with a few qualities of both.

Suzy tried. Sometimes, lying with my hands tied up and her smoldering gaze on me, she managed to bring me out of myself. And maybe it wasn't exactly how I wanted it to be, but she made the effort—and I could hardly expect her to be Leigh, who'd had the great advantage of unearthing this side of me, and making everything she did to me a shocking surprise. The effort she put in was enough for me for a long time because all other aspects of our relationship pleased me, and at least she wasn't afraid to talk about it. Perhaps that was the open-mindedness I'd recognized in her at Henderson's that day Troy left.

But now, in this hotel room in San Francisco, Suzy already half snoozing next to me, I can almost feel Leigh's presence. Or the promise of her presence. The way I did on nights when Troy was with his dad and I couldn't get to our apartment fast enough because I knew she'd be waiting for me—waiting to do her worst to me. And she always, always did. Like that day not long after my thirty-second birthday when she was waiting for me by the door.

"Give me your stuff, I'll put it away." She knew I wouldn't be able to relax if she just had me drop my coat to the floor. "Go into the bedroom, take off all your clothes. Don't lie down."

I hurriedly did what I was told and waited for her to join me, idly standing around, but not even touching the bed with my knee for support. I heard her shuffle around and then she walked in with her hands behind her back.

"I got you something, but you can't see, only feel." She had a wicked grin on her face. Back then, I hadn't told anyone yet what she did to me in the privacy of our bedroom. Not even Muriel. I just couldn't. I was afraid that some of the magic would go if I shared it. I was also still heavily processing the discovery of my own well-hidden needs. "On the bed. On all fours," she commanded. "Face away from me."

No kisses or other displays of affection had been exchanged yet. They would follow later. Softly and extensively. This always came first.

I crawled onto the bed and waited some more. I could hear Leigh put something on the chair next to the bed and remove some of her clothing.

By the time I felt her lean her weight against the bed, my clit was engorged, and I was ready. At least I thought I was.

She waited a few more seconds. I heard something rustle, felt her weight shift, and then nothing but excruciating, exquisite pain. Leigh had always spanked me with her hands, a belt, or a flogger up until now, not with… I didn't really know what it was. Only that its impact was wide and heavy and stung my cheeks like they would never recover.

I braced my body for the next blow, but to no avail. The pain crashed through me even harder, my flesh stung, and tears sprang from my eyes.

"Maybe you should count," she said, her voice emotionless.

Bam. She hit me again with what I was starting to believe was a paddle. "Three," I said.

"Oh no, no, no." I heard her huff out a disdainful breath. "Start from one."

I didn't know how many more of these I could take.

"One to ten. It's very simple," she said.

Ten more? Surely she couldn't be serious? Surely my ass was striped bright red already and well on the way to pleasing her.

She slapped me again, hitting only my left cheek. The pain vibrated through me, connecting with my clit. Wetness oozed from me. Before Leigh, I had absolutely no idea pain could feel this good. That, if someone pushed me the right way, I could take just about anything. Leigh had always known.

She alternated between my cheeks for number two and

three and paused for a few seconds before launching into number four, five, and six in quick succession.

By the time I had to say "Seven" my voice came out too muffled.

"Again, Jodie," she said. "And count properly so I can hear you."

Leigh was never one to show mercy. That's what I liked about her the most under these circumstances. The way I could always count on her to make me dig a little deeper, to look for an even greater rush of pleasure than the one I was growing accustomed to.

I counted out the last three blows, agony converting into excruciating bursts of pleasure in my flesh. Then, nothing again for a few long minutes. I didn't hear Leigh move and she didn't say anything. I knew she was admiring her work, something I reveled in even more. Her glance on my ass. I knew what would come next. Meanwhile, a thick, slow pulse had taken over my pussy lips, converging in my clit.

Where I had expected to feel her fingertips run over the tortured skin of my behind, I was startled by the sensation of something that was not made of flesh. Instinctively, I turned my head.

"Look ahead," was all Leigh said. "Or else." *Or else.* So much of what she triggered in me was based on the words 'or else'. And I was always ambivalent about them. Eager to please, but also curious as to what new heights they would take me. Sometimes, when I didn't obey, when I pushed boundaries, she saw through me and said, "I know what you're trying to do and that doesn't work on me." But, sometimes, she gave in and indulged me with another round of spanking, or an extra finger where I wasn't expecting it.

That day, I had no desire to determine what lay behind her 'or else' and I stared in front of me, at the curtains, of which the pattern was just a collection of smudges through my tears.

It only took me a minute to figure she was trailing the tip of a dildo over the curve of my behind. The only thing I didn't know was if it was one from our collection or a new toy. And if new, how wide and big it was.

I could hear her breathing become labored—just the tiniest display of losing composure. I never let on that I could tell from the speed of her breath when she was going to start fucking me. I kept it as a secret that served me well. As a tiny means of clinging on to a sense of control.

Soon after, the tip of the dildo reached my pussy lips. It slipped through easily.

"Spread wider," Leigh said and tapped my bottom with a few fingers. A gesture that normally wouldn't hurt, but brought tears to my eyes after the paddle strokes she had delivered earlier. I slid my knees as far apart as they would go.

Without further ado, she slid the toy inside of me. Gently at first, so I could get used to it, but it didn't take long for her thrusts to become bolder, demanding more of me. I felt the dildo's girth splay me open, but for Leigh, I always took it easily.

The skin of my behind burned, and the strokes she delivered with the toy touched me and filled me and satisfied me and I didn't need my clit to be touched. Leigh's mantra, almost from the very beginning, had always been, "Your clit is for quickies. I want to earn your climax." She never failed to do that.

Then, while fucking me savagely, she flicked her fingers against my ass again. Not hard, but with enough gentle force to have the pain re-ignite. It spread through me like wildfire. It started as pain but then changed into a stinging warmth, a blanket of delicious hurt covering me. She kept hitting the same spot with her fingers and with the dildo inside of me until all my thought processes crumbled and I was just a body being taken.

Everything around me turned to liquid heat and painful pleasure and the highest highs of abandon.

When I came, my muscles spasmed, clenching the dildo deep inside of me, and the pain radiating from my ass washed over me like a wave that cleansed me of everything that had accumulated in my brain since we last fucked.

After, Leigh hurried to my side, looked into my eyes briefly, before kissing the tears from my cheeks. We lay like that for a long time, until most of the pain had subsided, and all my tears had dried up. Afterward, she let me fuck her, but in a much more subdued way, because neither one of us needed it to be any other way.

Suzy's completely asleep now, and on the TV something is being set on fire. I change the channel, hoping to catch the last of the *L.A. Law* episode, but it's gone to a commercial break, and I'm not sure I should be watching it right now, what with the trip down memory lane I've already taken.

CHAPTER SEVENTEEN

"Will you please tell Jodie about us..."—I don't immediately know how to quantify my relationship with Troy—"...meeting up." By the time he's preparing for his final exams, more than two years after he first contacted me, we've been seeing each other almost every month. As it turned out, I *did* have spare time to bestow on another human being. Of course, these hours I spend with Troy can't be compared with courting a lover. Yet, I find myself anticipating our meetings, often in student bars in Berkeley where I stick out like a sore thumb. Because of what he represents in my life. A small part of Jodie. The more we see of each other, the more of Jodie I recognize in him. His sense of social justice, I gather, is much more evolved than his peers'.

"I don't know how she will react." Troy came into the city to meet me. I considered inviting him to my house, but something stopped me.

"I understand that." More than I let on. "But it doesn't mean she shouldn't know."

"What difference does it really make, Leigh?" He rips tiny

pieces off a paper napkin and fidgets with them endlessly. "Mom's in New York. You're here."

I don't know how to explain this to Jodie's son. I can't even properly explain it to myself. "It just feels wrong to do this behind her back."

He waves me off, as he's done so many times already. I try not to inquire about Jodie too much, but sometimes it happens without me thinking about it, or he blurts something out about her, and the conversation automatically meanders in that direction. More often than not, we just chit-chat, and on occasion, I find myself thinking we chat like, perhaps, a mother would with her son. Although that really is taking it too far, especially given what has happened between Troy's actual mother and me. But when you've sat up with a boy when he was seven and had the stomach flu, and when you've taken him to soccer practice, and spent hours with him assembling puzzles and Lego constructions, part of that lingers in your soul.

What would he have called me if I had stayed? There was one time when I had picked him up from school. We walked home together, Troy gesturing with his hands and telling me about his day in excited tones. I gave him my keys to open the front door because he'd forgotten his own set and it just came out. "Thanks, Mom," he said. I tried to ignore it as best I could, and Troy just went about the rest of his day, but later, after dark, when Troy was in bed, I told Jodie.

"Troy called me Mom today."

Jodie sat with her head thrown back against the armrest of the sofa. She'd had an emotionally exhausting day. Her head shot up. "I guess that was to be expected at some point."

"It doesn't bother you?"

"Of course not. Why would it?"

"Because I'm not his mother." It came out all wrong. It was not what I meant. Not really. Although it was the truth.

"So it bothers *you*?" Jodie pushed herself up.

"No, I just think it's confusing when he calls us both Mom."

"Fine. I'll talk to him."

That was the end of the conversation. Troy never called me Mom again. I never knew what Jodie said to him, but I always regretted not having the balls to talk to him myself. To inquire why he had called me that. If in his child's brain it had just been a logical consequence of me living with him, or more of a conscious decision. Or even a way to coax a reaction out of me.

"Is Jodie coming to your graduation?" When, at the end of his second year, Troy told me Jodie was traveling to San Francisco with Suzy and Rosie, my heart had skipped several beats. They would stay in the city for a few days. Did I wish for him to arrange something? I told him I needed to think about it. It would have been different if Jodie had come alone, or with only Rosie as a companion. The mention of Suzy, whose name only occasionally popped up in our conversations, made me decide against it. Unsure if I could bear sitting through polite conversation with Jodie and her new girlfriend, I didn't take Troy up on his offer.

"Not sure." Troy shrugs. "You know what Mom is like." Do I? Still? I know he's referring to money, though. It makes me think of the house I've just bought, all large and shiny and empty, with no one waiting for me in any of its many rooms. Jodie still lives in the barely-two-bedroom apartment we once shared, because it's rent-controlled and she probably can't afford to live anywhere else, has this boy as her son and Rosie as her daughter, and how is that for acquiring wealth?

———

Troy has finished his exams when he tells me Jodie and Suzy have broken up.

"Oh," is all I say at first. This time, I *have* invited him to my home and have even attempted to cook us a meal.

"You know what I think sometimes, Leigh?" Troy asks. He has changed so much since that first time we saw each other again almost three years ago. Gerald's easy self-assuredness shines through his actions much more. "I think she may still love you."

As a rule, I don't drink when I'm with Troy, but I open a bottle of red wine there and then. "Why would you think that?" I don't look at him while I drive a corkscrew into the cork of the bottle.

"It never works out with anyone else."

"That doesn't mean anything." I glance at him. At this boy who I have invited to my house and who is about to eat my interpretation of chicken parmigiana. "Do you mind if I have a glass of red tonight? Rough day and all that."

"Sure." He doesn't ask if he can have some, but sips from the Sprite I've poured him instead. He's twenty-two. We could share a drink, but I guess it doesn't feel right for either of us. "Why are you single, anyway?" he asks. We usually don't venture into this conversational territory. Troy has told me about a few girls he's dating, but his affairs never seem to last longer than a few weeks, and he never pours his heart out to me. He isn't the type.

I chuckle nervously. "I work too hard."

He shakes his head. "Mom works hard and she finds the time. Even Dad is with Elisa now, and he must work eighty hours a week."

"Yes, well, I work even harder."

"Don't you want to be with someone?"

"I do." God yes, I do. "But it's not that easy."

"Why? Because you're a lesbian?"

That question takes me aback more than any other. I take a few gulps of wine. "Is this a cross-examination, Counselor Dunn?"

"No, of course not." He fidgets with his fingers. He can never sit still for more than a second. "We're friends, right? I'm just curious."

"It's not because I'm a lesbian." I start preaching. "I just haven't really met anyone I've wanted to get serious about for a long time."

He seems to accept that as a valid answer. "Will you come to my graduation ceremony?"

My eyes widen. "If you want me to." Perhaps no one else will see it like that, but I do feel I should be there. Even though I don't really know how to define our relationship, we are, indeed, friends.

"I do. I really do." The intense sparkle in his eyes almost makes me well up.

"Promise me one thing, though." I consider another glass of wine. "If Jodie decides to come, which I suspect she will, you have to tell her about me before the ceremony. She needs to know, Troy." There's no way Jodie will miss her son's graduation.

"Fine. I promise." He glares at me from under his lashes, the same way Jodie used to. "Don't you want to know what happened with Suzy?"

"I'm not sure it's my place to ask." The question's been on the tip of my tongue since he told me.

"Mom dumped her. The same way she did with Amy. So, you know, now she's single once again."

What does he expect me to do with this information? "I'm sorry for her."

"Yeah, me too, I guess."

"How about some food?" Jodie is single again and there's a good chance I'll run into her in a few weeks' time. The prospect fills me with dread and hope at the same time.

"I'm starving," Troy says in the way only men his age can.

CHAPTER EIGHTEEN

The day before I fly first class with Gerald to San Francisco for my son's graduation ceremony, Suzy calls. Again.

"I don't have time for this," I say, rather harshly. "Rosie's ill." I regret my tone of voice instantly. None of this is Suzy's fault.

"Do you want me to stay with her while you go to Berkeley?" Suzy asks. We were together for almost four years and breaking the pattern of our familiarity has been difficult. Being a single mom again has been even more difficult.

"No, I'll ask Muriel."

"I'll happily do it," Suzy insists.

"It's better if you don't."

"Can I at least come and see her while you're gone?"

"I don't know." Admittedly, I don't know what is best for everyone involved in this situation. I do know Rosie would love to see Suzy. They've lived together for more than two years. From Suzy's incessant phone calls since we broke up, it's impossible for me not to know how much she misses Rosie— and me. I'd never pegged her for the über-clingy type. Another thought I instantly regret. It's just that by the time I had worked up the nerve to end our relationship, I was rather fed up with Suzy.

"I'll call you later, okay?" I need a break from this conversation. I need to think. And I need to pack and console Rosie, who has been looking forward to this trip for a very long time, but is now too sick to go.

"Please do," Suzy says, as if she expects me not to. She hangs up and I sigh with relief.

Staying with Suzy would definitely have been the easier option. Things were never bad between us. No blazing rows kept us awake at night. Ours was a silent, treacherous downfall. One that kept me awake at night nonetheless.

I go into Rosie's room to find her fast asleep. I put the back of my hand on her forehead. She still feels too warm. I've considered canceling my trip, but I have two children, and I haven't seen Troy in such a long time. Although he will be back in New York soon enough, I still think that, as his mother, I should be there for the ceremony. Perhaps I *should* allow Suzy to stay with Rosie. It would comfort her. But I have to think about the long-term consequences. If I let Suzy come over too much, Rosie will never get used to her moving out.

Hurting Rosie was, ultimately, what hurt me the most during this break-up. She had that same look on her face as Troy did when Leigh left. When will my mistakes stop repeating themselves, I wonder? I probably shouldn't date again until Rosie's old enough to understand that, sometimes, between grown-ups, things just don't work out.

I pass by the hallway mirror and ask myself, "What does that mean, though? Do you even understand?"

I glance back at my tired reflection. Good old Muriel will stay with Rosie. She and Francine love her to pieces. I won't even have to ask. All I will have to say is that Rosie won't be able to go with me to Berkeley, and she will offer to take care of her.

"That doesn't answer my question," I say to myself, like a woman who's about to lose her mind.

I had to break up with Suzy. It seemed that every day another personality trait of hers, one I had easily put up with for years, started grating on my nerves. Until it added up to me actively trying to avoid her.

The day before I asked her to leave I sat crying on Muriel's sofa. "It's really hard to explain, but it's like I've fallen completely out of love with her for no reason."

"There doesn't need to be a reason, Jodie. Sometimes two people only have a limited time together. Not everything is forever. That's just a fairy tale. And a conspiracy by the wedding industry."

"What about you and Francine?" I asked in between sniffles.

"We've just found a successful way of putting up with each other's shit. That's all. There's no magic."

"Then why can't I do that?"

"Because, sweetie, everyone is different."

"I don't understand," Suzy said. "What's wrong? We have a great life together. We're a family."

"I can't be with you anymore," I insisted. "It's not your fault." Try telling someone you've shared your life with for several years that you don't love them anymore without breaking their heart. "It's all me. You're not to blame."

"There must be something I can do." Suzy was a fighter. "Do you need some space? Some distance? I can go stay with Dave for a while, but don't do this, Jodie. Don't pull the plug on us like this." She was being very practical about it. I presumed the actual shock would come later.

"I've thought about this for a very long time." Months on end, I had mulled the inevitable decision over in my mind, on my way to work, on walks to court, en route to Rosie's school.

Could I not be a bit more lenient? Perhaps with time some of the old sparks would return? "And I'm sorry to say it's over." By the time I told her I was able to be quite matter-of-fact about it. I'd done my crying already. I'd already grieved for what we once had.

I had tried to explain it as calmly as possible. I'd arranged for Rosie to have a sleepover at her friend Gracie's house, and had knocked off work early so I was home before Suzy arrived. I wondered if saying the actual words might make me change my mind, but looking at Suzy's devastated face as I broke the news only reinforced the feeling that I should have done this months ago. But I was always waiting for a change, for a tidal wave of magic to make things better. To make me a better person. Someone who loved their partner for eternity.

"That's all you have to say?" Suzy asked. "After four years? After I've taken care of your child like she was my own." I thought it a low blow to involve Rosie in this situation, but I understood.

"I'm sorry."

"But... what have I done wrong?"

"Absolutely nothing." There was no relief to be found in this moment. I knew both of our lives would get worse for a while until they got better. "You can stay for as long as you need to. We will tell Rosie together."

Suzy shook her head in disbelief. "I'm not staying in a house where I'm not wanted." Then she started to cry. Not hysterically. She had too much self-respect for that. "Is it sex?" she asked, sort of out of the blue. "I've tried to comply with your wishes as best I could, and I know that's why it didn't work out with you and Amy."

"No, Suze, no." Of course, sex had something to do with it, but that most certainly wasn't Suzy's fault. And I had learned my lesson after Amy—and altered my expectations accordingly. *It's just, when I try to imagine myself a few years from now, there's no scenario in which I can picture you by my side.* I didn't say that out loud because I considered it too cruel.

Perhaps she had come into my life at a time when I needed someone most. There was so much comfort to be found in falling in love with Suzy Henderson. I was in love with her, but then it faded, and everyday life mundanity took over until I felt I had nothing left to hold on to.

"Couples go through phases," she said next. "It can't always be good."

"It's not a phase." That sentence reminded me of what I'd told Gerald when I finally figured out that it was a woman I wanted to be with.

And now here I stand. My spirits low because of the break-up and how badly Suzy is taking it. Because my little girl can't see her brother graduate. But also with an undefined flutter in my stomach, because I'm flying to San Francisco. To Leigh's city.

CHAPTER NINETEEN

I can feel Jodie's eyes on the back of my head, like a rifle's laser sights. I told Troy over and over again that, if he didn't tell his mother about us seeing each other, it would be a bad idea for me to attend his graduation, but he was adamant. He wanted me there. He even said that, if it hadn't been for me, he might not even be graduating, but I saw through that one easily. He was just being dramatic.

He only told me yesterday that he hadn't been able to work up the nerve to tell Jodie about our friendship.

"I should have told her years ago," he said, "now it feels like I've been doing something bad."

I'm afraid to move. I stand here as though my neck is stuck in a medical brace and I can only look straight ahead. I know Jodie's a few rows behind me with Gerald. No sign of Rosie. It's as if I can feel them talking about me. I can imagine what's going on inside Jodie's head right now. She must be furious because what right do I have to be here on this day? If only Troy had told her.

It's Troy's turn on the podium, and even though it's probably inappropriate, a ripple of pride runs through me when he waves from the stage. His wave is not aimed at me, of course, it's for his parents, but then he does glance in my direction, and I can't help myself, I turn around and locate Jodie in the crowd instantly, as though my vision is a radar trained to only ever find her. I smile. She doesn't smile back. Then she shakes her head.

My heart is in my throat. Perhaps I should just leave. Pretend this moment never happened. But I can't just walk away from Jodie. Not again. Not now that I've actually seen her.

I patiently wait for the rest of the students to be called to the stage and have their moment. Every time one passes, my heart starts beating faster.

After the official part of the ceremony has ended, I watch Troy as he heads in Jodie and Gerald's direction. Should I just walk up to them? After having seen Jodie shake her head at me like that? As if that gesture could erase my being here.

I take a few steps toward them. I'm not just going to stand here as if I don't belong. Troy and I have a relationship now, and I'm here for him. Although I've been on edge since the day he asked me to attend. The prospect of seeing Jodie, which would be inevitable, caused a few more sleepless nights than I had expected.

"Mom, I hope you don't mind I invited Leigh," I hear Troy say. His voice is that of a man who knows he's guilty. "I didn't really know how to tell you, but we've been seeing quite a bit of each other." *Good one, Troy,* I think. *Lay it on her here and now.* Inwardly, I roll my eyes. But if you can't do stupid things when you're young, when can you? He beckons for me to join them. I paint a confident smile on my face.

"Jodie." I don't really know what else to say. "It's been too long." I don't know what to do either. Standing face-to-face with her has me reduced to a brainless creature. I extend my hand. Troy has to nudge her in the elbow before she shakes it.

The meeting of our palms is quick and awkward. I decide to direct my attention to her ex-husband.

"Gerald. How have you been?"

"Truth be told, I hadn't expected to see you here today." He ignores my question, but focusing my attention on him allows me to regain some of my wits.

"Troy wants to go to law school. Who's he gonna call, right?"

"I've learned so much from Leigh already, Mom," Troy says. Oh, christ. That boy sure knows how to push Jodie's buttons. "Can she come to dinner with us?" he asks.

I have to step in. I also don't particularly feel like having dinner with Gerald. "That's quite all right, Troy," I interject. "I'll take you out some other time." I shoot Jodie a quick, apologetic glance.

"For old times' sake, I guess," Jodie says. A shudder of something—Satisfaction? Nerves? Guilt?—rushes through me. Gerald doesn't look too pleased about his ex-wife's impromptu decision.

"Awesome," Troy says, holding up his hand for a high-five. I don't care how silly it looks, and I slap my palm against his with a big burst of inexplicable joy coursing through me.

"See you at eight at Rudy's," Troy says to me. "I'll call ahead to let them know there'll be four of us instead of three." He pulls me into a hug. Afterward, I can't help but glance at Jodie again. The years have changed her, of course, but she's still Jodie. I think of that night after Karen broke up with me, and I tried to call her. What would have happened if she had picked up? And what is seeing me so unexpectedly doing to her? Despite Gerald's presence, I'm glad I'll get to spend some time with her.

"I believe you've earned yourself a beer, buddy," Gerald says to Troy.

I wasn't expecting that move from Gerald either. He's

giving me an opening here. I have to take it. "I know a great coffee place a few blocks from here," I say to Jodie. "Catch up?" My heart is almost bursting out of my chest. Seeing her makes my insides churn with nerves but, at the same time, joy sparks within me, and it seems to multiply by the second.

"Why not?" Jodie replies, but she looks at Troy, as though she's doing *him* a favor. He hugs her in response.

"Thanks, Mom." He lets go of Jodie and addresses Gerald. "Come on, Dad. I know just the place."

Jodie and I stand in silence for a while.

"How about something stronger than coffee?" she asks, finally meeting my gaze.

"Oh yes." I can actually feel my confidence coming back, like a coat I had misplaced, but found again and it still fits me like a glove. "Come on, we'll take my car."

I drive us to the same place where I first met Troy again. We manage to find a table on the back patio and we both order martinis—dirty with two olives—the way we used to.

"You're at a considerable advantage here, Leigh. You knew you would see me today. You had time to prepare. Whereas I, frankly, am still recovering from the shock," Jodie says as soon as the waiter goes back inside.

"It's just a conversation, Jodes. There are no advantages or disadvantages to be had." I didn't mean to call her by her nickname. It just came out.

"Christ, always the lawyer," she says awkwardly.

"But you're right. I've known for a while that I'd be seeing you—and I've been nervous about it ever since." I can't wait for that drink to arrive, although I must not overindulge. I'm driving Jodie, after all. How long has that been? Since we drove to The Hamptons for the very last time. The drive back to the city from The Hamptons has managed to stay lodged in my memory despite its blurry, dreamlike quality. Two hours of my brain playing ping-pong.

"I know you hated me for a long time after, Jodes. That weighed heavy on me. I wish we could have had a cleaner break—" Oh no, I said it again.

"There are no clean breaks when so much love is at stake." Jodie's tone is harsh.

"I know, but at the time, it was the only way for me. I hope you can see that now."

"No need to revisit. You made your reasons very clear. Sometimes, it just doesn't work out."

I can't help but shake my head. "Don't give me that. The end of our relationship was not a matter of 'it not working out.'" Finally the waiter returns. "It was a matter of wanting totally different things from life."

"I don't see the difference, but if you say so," Jodie says.

"We were right for each other on so many levels." I take a few quick sips. I need them.

"And yet here we are. Sipping martinis like virtual strangers."

"I wish it didn't have to be like that." I take a bigger gulp now. "I wish you didn't feel the need to be so defensive."

"That's a good one coming from the woman who, in all of my life, broke through my walls the most." Jodie hesitates for a second. "I had no choice but to build them back up again after we broke up. Doubly fortified."

"I couldn't stay, Jodie. It would have made us both miserable."

She nods. We both know. "Are you, huh,"—she pauses again—"seeing someone?"

"Not at the moment." Not for a long time, I think. "If I were, she wouldn't be too happy I'm meeting up with you."

"How do you mean?" Jodie's green gaze rests on me.

"Because no one else ever lived up to you. To what we had together." In a way, it's a relief to finally be able to say this. Not to anyone else, but straight to Jodie's face. "Obviously, I didn't realize that at the time."

"Regrets?" Jodie asks. Her spine is straight, but her voice wavers a bit.

"It's hardly fair to sit here now and claim that I regret my decision, after all this time. Let's just say that, on a personal level, my life didn't exactly work out as I had planned."

"As opposed to it doing so brilliantly on a professional level?"

"I'm good at my job. Always have been. But it came at a cost."

"We all have a price to pay."

"You have Troy and Rosie. No price is big enough for that."

"That might be true." She looks away from me. "Doesn't mean I didn't miss you terribly."

"Comes with the territory of breaking up." My glass is almost empty.

The ringing of Jodie's phone interrupts our conversation. She grabs for it hastily in her bag.

"Tonight?" I hear her say without hiding the disappointment in her voice.

"It's okay, honey." *Honey?* Who is she talking to? Rosie? "You'll be in New York most of the summer. We can celebrate for weeks on end." It must be Troy. Is he canceling their—and my—dinner plans? Hope flares in my chest. More of Jodie just for me.

"Yes. Just catching up…" Jodie says before hanging up and staring at her phone indecisively.

"Stuck with me?" I ask, unable to mask the twinge of hope in my tone.

"Looks like it." Jodie looks at me and I can tell—I still can—she's not too unhappy about this situation.

"I'm not going to lie, Jodie. I love Troy to pieces, but that ex-husband of yours, well… I'm glad I got out of that particular dinner. Imagine the riveting conversation. I'd much rather spend the evening with you." I don't hold back when I stare at her. "That is, if you want to, of course."

"If I had known my son would ditch me, I would have booked the red-eye back to New York. Rosie has the flu. Poor thing." She's lost in thought for an instant. "I hated that I had to leave her behind this weekend, but I couldn't do that to Troy. And she's in good hands with Muriel."

"Troy has shown me pictures of her. What a cute little thing. And quite the mouth, I hear?"

"It's a rewarding thing, you know, motherhood. Hard to put into words. But we're all different, I guess." Jodie's tone has gone hard again.

"Do you really want to go there again?" I slant my body over the small table. "Or do you want to enjoy the few hours we have together tonight? I, for one, am very happy to see you. And I've never blamed you for the choices you made, despite the fact that all they came down to was that there was no longer room for me in your life." I lean in a little closer. "And don't, not even for a split second, think it didn't hurt me every bit as much as it did you."

She holds up her hands, displaying her palms.

"How about another drink?" I smile at her, hoping to convey that she should say yes.

"Sure."

I hold up my hand to signal the waiter. "Tell me about Suzy," I ask, although I have no right to.

"What did my son have to say about her?"

"We never gossip about you in that way, Jodie. I promise. We both respect you too much for that. Anyway, Troy claimed he never really got to know her."

"You ruined me for a lot of women." A grin breaks on Jodie's lips.

"Oh sure, blame me." I grin back. "Any other woman would thank me, by the way."

"As I'm sure many have."

"Ha." I feign indignation. "I'll admit that for a while after we broke up and I moved West, I played the field. But, as you well know, I've never really been one for one-night stands and affairs going nowhere. I need more than that. Much more."

"Only total surrender."

"Oh, Jodie." I can't stop looking at her. All these years of not being with her, not experiencing what only she has ever given me. "Tell me what you're thinking right now." I can't be a hundred percent sure of the quickly changing vibe between us, but I take a chance, anyway.

"I'm too old for your games now, Leigh," she says, but I can tell she's at least a little bit interested. I can tell by how she flutters her lashes and fiddles with the cuff of her blouse.

"It was worth a try."

"Was it?" She looks at my hands. Perhaps she remembers what they can do.

"Where are you staying?" I need to make my move now. "I'm only asking because I'd much rather do something else with you than sit here and get drunk."

"You remember well." Jodie cocks her head.

"'Fondly' would be a better word for it." I empty my drink. "Back in the day you were much quicker to say yes."

"What can I say? I was thirty years old and still so easily impressed."

"Hm. I disagree." I eye her glass, hoping it will make her empty it quicker. "I think, that particular day, what you needed more than anything, was for someone to sweep you off your feet."

"Cut to Leigh Sterling, who did a sterling job."

"We were such different people then."

"What kind of person are you now, though, I wonder?" Jodie asks.

"Evidently not the kind who can persuade you to invite me to your hotel with one well-aimed, smoothly delivered sentence. Not anymore."

"You're so much more than that. Always were."

"I'm not playing games right now, Jodie." I can hear the urgency in my voice. "What would you like to do? I feel like we have this chance here, time for something unexpected… to get reacquainted, perhaps. I don't know." I shake my head. "As far as relationships go in my life, ours still counts as the most significant one I've ever had."

"Is Troy setting me up in some way? Obviously, he wanted me to see you again. And that whole basketball game excuse he just called me about… is he playing lawyer tricks on me?"

"I don't know, but does it really matter?" The joy I experienced earlier is soon making way for a slew of painful memories.

"Did you ask him to arrange this?"

"I would never use your son like that." This time I don't have to feign indignation. "We may well be sitting here together with a whole evening stretched out in front of us because he wanted it, but if that's the case, it's his doing alone. Not mine." I swallow hard. "You're also free to go whenever you want."

She holds up her palms again. "This is emotional for me, too."

"I know. I shouldn't have said that, it's just…" I tilt my head and find her eyes. "I hadn't expected you to have this effect on me, still."

"Let's go to my hotel," Jodie says suddenly.

I don't say anything, just call for the waiter. Jodie leaves some money on the table, and before I fully realize what is happening, I'm driving us to the hotel where Jodie is staying.

CHAPTER TWENTY

When we step into the elevator, I half-expect Leigh to start kissing me, but this is eleven years later, and all the boundaries we once carefully set have vanished, and when I look at myself in the shiny metal of the door, I see a different woman—outside and in. Yet, I want her to. I want someone to do that to me again. To take away all the things that always simmer somewhere in the back of my brain, to take away that longing that's been building in my gut for years. And I only want Leigh to do it. She's no means to an end. She's my ex-partner. The only one who ever knew me well enough to take me to the place I needed to go. Because the things I want, you don't just ask of someone. Or, at least, I guess you could, but it would take away half the pleasure.

The elevator cabin is silent, apart from a buzzing hum, and the sound of our breath, coming as regularly as always. Yet, beneath my skin, my blood is sizzling. I start making up a list of all the things this is not, but I realize quickly that I don't need to. I don't need to overthink this, or think about it at all. That's the whole point of inviting her to my room.

The best part of this entire elevator ride, which is about to come to an end, is that I get to experience both sides of the thrill. I know Leigh and the familiarity between us reassures me, yet I haven't seen her in years and there's the excitement of newness crashing through my flesh as well. Do I still love her? I ask myself as we exit the elevator and I guide her to my room in the furthest corner of the hallway. Do I? If I do, it's in a totally different way than before. The love that remains after the hurt has been dealt with. A more sedated, stable kind of affection based on memories and shared experiences and the life we once lived together. But, no matter what we do or how hard we try, we can never, ever get that life back.

As soon as we walk into my room—the one Gerald has generously paid for—which is swanky and large and boasts full-length windows on one side, Leigh starts scanning her surroundings. The curtains will have to remain open, of that I'm sure already, but she's also looking for props. I wonder if I would be offended if she unearthed some sort of toy from her bag, a flogger perhaps, or handcuffs. If I would be able to forgive such presumptuousness. But not even Leigh Sterling can rise to that level of audacity, and I remember what she used to say to me. "You have no idea what you give me when you take the pain." But I did, and I still do.

"Drink?" I ask.

"Just some water, please." To my surprise, Leigh dodges my glance when I look at her.

"Are you okay?" I try to make my question sound casual as I snatch a bottle of water from the minibar and pour its contents into a wine glass.

"I don't know." Is she having second thoughts? What was I expecting anyway? A re-run of our first date? "I think I know what you want from me, but I can't read you like that anymore. Too much time has passed." She takes the glass I hand her and deposits it on the desk she's leaning against. "I'm also not sure we are people who can just do this once and walk away, especially with the history we share. I'm only speaking for myself, of course. But this, for me, can never be casual. Not with you."

"What are you trying to say?" My heart is thumping away beneath my ribs. I grab the tiny bottle of Scotch I took from the minibar earlier and start to unscrew the top. Are we not on the same page, after all?

"I *do* have regrets. What if you *were* the one I let go? After you, my life did not become what I wanted it to be, and you know why? Because, yes, I'm good in court, and I was made partner well before I turned forty-five, and I made much more money than I could ever spend, because what would I possibly spend it on? Myself? I'm always working, anyway, because when I come home at night, to my gorgeous house, no one's there."

The person standing in front of me is so far removed from the Leigh I expected to encounter in my hotel room, I need to blink. "Why don't we sit for a bit?" I gesture at two club chairs flanking the window.

"I'm sorry, Jodie. I know this is not what you signed up for." Leigh sighs when she crashes into the chair, and there's nothing regal about her posture anymore. It reminds me of the day we broke up. She looked like her spine had shrunk several inches, and her voice had lost all of its liveliness. Leigh never had to tell me she was hurting, I always knew well before she had the nerve to fess up.

"I didn't sign up for anything." I sit down opposite her, trying to find her eyes, but she keeps looking away. "You're a bit young for a midlife crisis." I try a joke.

"It's you." The words come out as a whisper. "I usually don't feel like this. Perhaps because I don't allow myself to. Or because I don't have time for self-pity, but mainly because I'm not the type to dwell and look back like this on the choices I've made. But seeing you... actually, if I'm being truly honest, it started when Troy contacted me for the first time. That kid."

She shakes her head. "I could have been there for all of it—his first girlfriend, his first year in high school, his first everything—but I walked away."

"Please stand up," I ask, leading by example. I extend my hand and wait for her to take it. She does, letting her fingers brush over mine before truly grasping them, and pulling herself up.

"If I were you, I'd kick me out as well." A hint of a smile breaks through the sadness on her face.

"I'm not kicking you out." *I always wanted you to stay*, I think, but don't say out loud. "Who knows why we make the choices we make, Leigh? All we know is that they make us into the person we're meant to become. You're a hot-shot lawyer now, which is, by the way, quite a sexy thing to be. You know, in an Amanda Donohoe eighties kind of way." At last, the first hint of her trademark grin. "You're only forty-five. And as you just said, you're not someone who looks back often, so look to the future. One of the big advantages of the life you've lived so far is that you have no strings attached. You can be or do whatever you want."

Leigh's grip around my fingers grows firmer, yet I'm the one who leans forward and instigates the first kiss. "For example, you can do this." I tip my head and inhale her scent before pressing my lips to hers. I wish I could say her scent roused a million memories from my soul, but I've given birth to another child since she left, I've lived a whole new life, and the smell of my ex-lover is as new to me as all the rest of this.

"I need to know how *you* feel," Leigh says, as we pull back from what I can hardly describe as the passionate lip-lock I had hoped for.

"How I feel?" Despair clings to my voice. "Confused, horny, ready…" I ramble. "I want you, Leigh. That's how I feel."

"You want me for the person I once was to you." Leigh brings her face closer again. "You want me to tie you to that bedpost over there"—her eyes dart away from me for a moment—"and push five fingers inside of you."

It's exactly what I want, but I'm not sure I should just give myself away like that. It doesn't really work that way—never has.

"Most of all," Leigh continues, "you want me to stop talking." Her eyes bore into mine, and I can tell she's getting there, that she's getting herself ready. "And take charge."

Almost imperceptibly, I nod, and I feel everything falling away. The years we haven't seen each other, the pain we caused each other that has colored our memories, and, perhaps in both of our cases, altered our view on life as well. Because isn't our life made up of the people that we love? The people that have the power to fundamentally change something about us? Apart from my children, no one has ever had as profound an effect on me as Leigh Sterling. She knows it too. I see it in the way her facial expression is changing. Eyes that seem to look straight into my soul. That knowing, lopsided smile. Even in the way she tilts her head, exposing the length of her neck, as ever, a question in the slant of it: are you ready?

In a flash, her hands are on the back of my neck, pulling me in. The kiss that follows is much more invasive. There's nothing exploratory or cautious about it. It's a declaration of intent. The way Leigh claims me with her tongue now is how she'll claim me with her fingers later.

When we break from the kiss, I already feel out of breath and my knees are giving way. Not even the best sex I had with Suzy comes close to this thirty-second kiss from my ex. Apples and oranges. There's no use comparing the two.

CHAPTER TWENTY-ONE

"You'd better undress and bend over," I tell Jodie. She obeys instantly, just as she used to.

I keep my glance on her while she unbuttons her blouse and lets it drop to the carpet. Eleven years ago, Jodie would never have just discarded a piece of clothing like that.

When only her underwear remains, she pauses. I arch up my eyebrows, just as a matter of encouragement. The years have changed her body—how could they not? I hope she can tell that I think she's as beautiful as ever from the way I'm looking at her.

She unclasps her bra, hesitates for a moment before dropping it, then quickly takes off her panties as well.

"You know the pose." I move out of her way, wondering if she still does.

She bends over and presents her ass to me.

I'm momentarily floored by how easy she's making it on me, and by how she still seems to trust me after all these years. Maybe, when you love the way we did, it never really goes away. Maybe something lingers, the way people can survive with a piece of shrapnel in their body after an accident. It hurts. And it's an almost constant reminder. But survive they do.

I look at Jodie's behind in silence a few seconds longer. I know what that does to her. I also know what it does to me.

I quickly remove my blouse and then trace a finger up the curve of her ass. I feel her flinch underneath my touch. I can't lift my finger from her skin. I run it up and down her cheeks, reacquainting my fingertip with this body that has given me so much pleasure.

When I'm finally able to drag my finger away from her flesh I suck it into my mouth, as though it's the quickest way to savor her. I also know where my finger is going next, and some moistness wouldn't go amiss.

The fragility I displayed earlier leaves me, and I bring my finger to her behind again. Let her feel it's good and wet so she can draw her own conclusions about where this is going. And I fully realize this is going very fast, but there's no other way for Jodie and me to do this. Falling into bed smiling, caressing each other until the next morning, that was never how we did things —except perhaps for the first few times we made love, when I hadn't fully gauged her yet.

My finger inches closer to her crack. Oh, to be able to see her face right now. That face I've missed so much, that I've conjured up from memory many a night over the past eleven years. Those green eyes. Those long lips with their color of bruised plums—still her favorite lipstick. I was always sure a deeper meaning lay behind it, but if it did, she never admitted to it.

Has anyone else done this to her? Has Suzy ventured here? I can't help but wonder these things, but, as far as I know, she's not stayed with anyone longer than with me.

I only apply gentle pressure, just so she knows what to

expect. And this image in front of me, Jodie offering herself to me like this, it's so *us* it brings a tear to my eye.

"Get up," I say, making sure no sentimentality shows in my voice.

Jodie pushes herself up and a smile flits along her lips when she sees I've taken off my blouse. Her eyes stop at my abs. I have a fully fitted gym in my house. It's not as if I needed the room for my offspring, I want to say, but it would be a joke in extremely bad taste.

"Face the window," I instruct.

While she does, I unbuckle my belt.

"Hands on the glass, ass out." Jodie was always coy about doing it in front of the window, but when I let a finger drift along her pussy lips I could always tell how much it aroused her.

She's gasping for air already and it's as if I can tell by the tautness of her muscles and the eagerness of her breath that no one has demanded this of her in years.

Our eyes meet in the reflection of the window.

"Let's give them a show," I say, and move behind her. With a fingertip, I mark the spot where I will slap her. I easily remember where it always used to hurt her the most.

I let the leather of my belt crash down on the spot I traced. Jodie's body jerks.

"Fuck," she hisses, and her hands slide down the window a few inches.

I know what she needs to get over the bite of the first slap. Another. The sound of the leather cracking on her skin injects jolt after jolt of fireworks into my blood. It's not as if I haven't done this with other women. Karen comes to mind, but it was never the same. I was Jodie's first. We made this happen together and created something between us that can, quite possibly, withstand eleven long years of absence.

"Mmm," I groan, just to give her a little something to hold on to. A tiny sign of approval.

Whack. I treat Jodie's other butt cheek to the same, but instead of just two strokes, I let them come down hard and fast. Asking her to count now would be beyond cruel.

One last crack of my belt and the reflection of her face in the window gives me a lump in my throat. I haven't been faced with such surrender in a long time. So much of what we had between us is still there. It rose to the surface the instant my belt connected with her flesh.

And I want to grab her, kiss her, tell her all the things I've saved up over the years, but I need to end this ritual properly. I let my finger trace the marks my belt has left, rubbing the pain into her flesh even more. Nobody has ever hurt for me the way Jodie has.

Then I can't stop myself from taking her into my arms any longer. I glue my body to her backside and the contact of our skins nearly makes me cry. Nearly.

"Is that what you wanted, Jodie?" I ask. I feel her body give a little in my embrace. "Answer me." I find her gaze in the window's reflection.

"Yes," she says, her voice hoarse.

"On the bed," I command, but I find myself unable to step away from her—I've done enough of that in my life. Instead of making room for her to move, I press my nose into her hair and inhale her scent.

At last, I give her the space she needs to turn around, but still I can't fully find the persona I usually so easily adopt in the bedroom. I grab her by the back of the neck and kiss her deeply. I recover quickly, as if a little bit of her is enough for now, and end our kiss abruptly.

"Go on," I say, not allowing for any more hesitation. "You know the drill."

By the time I've stripped off the rest of my clothes, Jodie is in position on the bed. She lies on her back, her fingers curled around the railing.

I loop the belt I used on her earlier and fasten it around her wrists nice and tight.

"Spread your legs." I crawl to the back of the bed and take in the sight. Her pussy lips glisten with moisture, and I can't let her know how seeing her like this affects me. "Wider," I say in a stern voice. She lets her knees fall farther to either side.

"You really want this, don't you?" I can't look away from Jodie's pussy. I can hardly stand the thought that other women have touched it, but I know it's a highly hypocritical, useless thought. "You want to be fucked so badly, don't you, Jodie?" I tear my gaze away from between her legs and look her in the eyes.

"Yes." Her tone is more defiant than I had expected. Time to take her down a peg.

"How many fingers, Jodie?" I ask. "Three?" I chuckle. "Nah, three is nothing for you. I know that much. Four perhaps?" I let my gaze drop down to between her legs again. "Or do you want everything, Jodie? Hm?"

"All of it," she rumbles, her breath ragged.

"Are you sure?"

"Yes," she says, like the first time she asked me to do this to her. I haven't reached the exact headspace I need for this yet. Maybe this was the way it was destined to go between us this afternoon, but it doesn't mean it's easy. This is as far removed from just sex—from just two bodies meeting—as I've ever been. All the memories, the regrets, the mistakes that lie between us, and yet, look at us now. I'm about to fuck her, give her everything, and I feel nerves rage in my belly.

"Yes," she says, her eyes on me. "And you know it."

I put a hand on Jodie's lower belly and I can hear her breath catch in her throat. I marvel at how her skin breaks out in goosebumps at the slightest touch of my hand. I look up and see impatience glitter in her eyes. Perhaps she has waited for this moment as long as I have. My waiting was never entirely conscious, except in those rare moments when I got completely hammered on martinis and, as they say, the truth just lay there, all bare and obvious for me to see at the bottom of my glass. I could hardly describe those as conscious moments, though. Only fleeting instances of longing that passed when the next day came and the new morning light erased them.

I guide my fingers to her cunt. No hesitation. I need to be inside of her now. Three slip in easily. Jodie gasps for air but doesn't close her eyes, and that's when I truly see her. A state of abandon is not that hard to reach when you know how to push someone's buttons, but this is not just abandon on Jodie's face. I halt the motion of my fingers, just let them be inside of her, all of Jodie clasping around them while I look into those green, green eyes. And I already know there will be no walking away from this. Those eyes, that glare, even the new lines that have gathered around her mouth, they're my home. Three seconds inside of Jodie is all I need to know that, eleven years ago, I made a big mistake.

I start fucking her and she groans in response.

"Oh fuck," she says. "Oh, Leigh."

Hearing Jodie say my name unravels something inside of me, but I need to stay focused. I fuck her quicker, before pulling out and giving her everything she asked for. Slowly, slowly, I cover my hand in her wetness, and I fuck her with everything I have. Not just my hand, but my entire being. I should have known when I walked away from her after our last fuck, on the floor of her apartment. I broke down in Sonja's spare bedroom as soon as I deposited the suitcases Jodie had packed. I howled from sheer physical pain, but I thought that was normal. I was so utterly convinced I'd made the right decision, and it *was* the right decision at the time, but only for a brief while. I should have gone to see her when Muriel cornered me. I should have reversed our fate when I had the chance.

Jodie's eyes are glazing over. "Relax," I say because I have something else in store for her. What I hinted at earlier. I slip my free hand from her belly to beneath the hand I'm fucking her with. Jodie's eyes widen. She knows. Her eyes close.

I push my hand deeper into her pussy, while I circle her sphincter with the index finger of my other hand. I have to look away from her face. I need to see what my hands are doing.

I also can't look at her when I start to cry.

I let my finger slip past the rim and I can't help but sneak a glance. Tears run down Jodie's cheeks as well. Her eyes flicker open and shut, but I don't think she sees anything. She's lost in the moment and, perhaps, this is the sight I missed the most. The sight of total surrender. Her wrists bound. Her body completely open to me, a display of trust, a vision of what years apart can't erase.

I can feel her pussy starting to contract around my fist. Her body stiffens, then relaxes. Time for my hand to retreat, to leave Jodie Whitehouse—this time, it won't be forever.

Our eyes meet and Jodie seems taken aback by my tears. But all I see are my desires reflected back at me. We both knew well before entering this room that this would not be an ending again. I untie her wrists, massaging and kissing them where my belt dented the skin.

"Good grief, Jodie," I whisper in her ear as I push her down and stretch next to her.

Jodie wraps her arms around me and faces me. Our cheeks are sodden with tears of relief and nostalgia and—I know this —love. I hold her tight, hoping it comes across that I intend to never let her go again.

"Maybe you should come to New York sometime," Jodie says. My heart flutters. I don't know how to reply with words. I need to let a burst of happiness wash over me before I can find them.

"Maybe I will," I say, gravely understating my true emotions, but Jodie knows. I know she does.

CHAPTER TWENTY-TWO

The next morning when I wake up early because we never did take the time to draw the curtains, Leigh is still fast asleep beside me. I take in her relaxed face; her lips are slightly parted, her eyes a bit baggy from the crying.

I check the alarm clock and my first thought, as always, is Rosie. It's only 6 a.m. Gerald and I will meet Troy for breakfast at 9 so we can catch the midday flight to New York.

Would it make Troy happy to see me appear at breakfast with Leigh by my side? It's a thought I'm not ready to entertain just yet.

Last night, Leigh and I got caught up in long hours of reminiscing, lying in each other's arms while avoiding drawing conclusions. Until we fell asleep, naked, our arms lightly touching, just as they always used to. What should my first words be to her when she wakes up? I can't stop looking at her. Her hair is pointing in all directions and one cheek is a bit wrinkly from lying on her side. It reminds me of lazy Sunday mornings when it was Gerald's week with Troy, and an entire day stretched out in front of us. The immense feeling of comfort to be spending the day with someone you love, doing the things you love, unencumbered, free in the union we then, still, chose.

My wrists are stiff, despite Leigh's incessant stroking of them last night, after the fact. When I stretch, my butt cheeks sting in the most satisfying way, and my pussy feels tender. I think of the time we have left, the few hours between now and my leaving for the airport. Would she really consider visiting me in New York? If all the things she said last night are true, she just might.

As much as I love watching her sleep, time ticking away from us gets the best of me. Leigh's lying on her back, the duvet half thrown off, and I remember what it was like to wake up beside her every morning. A small but significant blessing, because what better way to start the day than laying eyes on the woman I love? The woman who taught me more about myself than I ever deemed possible. After she left me, waking up was always the hardest—especially on days when Troy was at his dad's. But I've dealt with the emptiness of those mornings. Time has, for once, softened the memories that needed it most. And look at me now? Mother of two children, *and* in bed with Leigh Sterling. The most crucial of our differences dissolved as the years have gone by.

I trail a finger along her collarbones, only hesitating for a split second before dragging it down across her torso, to her left nipple. It's still limp with sleep, but not for long. I encircle it with the tip of my finger, but I need more. I move so I can take it in my mouth. As I wrap my lips around it, Leigh expels a light groan, followed by, "Good morning to you too."

Her voice instantly undoes me a little—although sparingly used, it was always an important instrument in our lovemaking—and I let her nipple slip from my lips to look at her.

"Morning." Leigh's face breaks into a smile that makes my heart sing. A grin so unselfconscious and free, it makes me realize I could fall in love with her all over again. "You should probably do it, you know," I hear myself say.

"What?" Leigh pulls me close to her, until my ear reaches her lips. "Book a ticket to New York, you mean?" Her voice is a horny whisper, full of promise of things to come—if she does book that ticket.

I nod, my cheek now against her lips. I turn my face toward her fully, to look into her eyes. No more words are needed now. I lean in to kiss her, and this kiss, this morning, with early sunlight illuminating us, and the memory of last night in our hearts, is one that travels all the way through me, its divine sensation settling in the pit of my stomach. I won't fall in love with Leigh again because I already am. Perhaps it started when she loosened her belt from her trousers—although that would mean reducing the moment to one of pure physicality. To the mere promise of sexual satisfaction, and it was so much more than that. If I know one thing, back in the day and now, it was never promises keeping us together. And it was never just the scorching scenes in our bedroom Leigh managed to create. It was—is—much more than that. Then and now. Because how do you forget a love like that? The life we shared, the companionship, the deep friendship and understanding that connected us much more than Leigh tying me up ever could, they were the hardest to lose.

How Leigh was there for me after rough days—and in my profession, a lot of days are heartbreaking—not just with legal advice and a shoulder to lean on, but how she knew the right, lighter words to say to cheer me up. How she could disarm me by arching up her eyebrows and pulling her lips into a silly grin. How, when I came home, I'd find her building an intricate Lego construction with Troy, his whole being so in awe of her—and how I felt that too, then.

"How about next weekend?" Leigh asks when we break from our kiss.

My bruised pussy lips are pulsing again and, despite knowing I need some time to recover, I already want her again. I feel it in every bone of my body. Leigh is inventive, she'll find a way to give me what I need. She always did.

"Can't wait," I say, as I feel tears stinging behind my eyes. Because this love of ours is greater than time. It's greater than the sacrifices we felt we needed to make. The sum of it is more than our separate desires. Maybe we didn't see it then, but I clearly see it now.

"I'll stay at the Library Hotel. I love that place," Leigh says.

"Nuh-uh." I shake my head. "You're staying with me."

"If you insist," she says.

"I do." I lean in for another kiss, and I can already see it. Leigh waking up in the bed we used to share. The four of us going for breakfast because Troy will be home from college. Rosie will have a million questions to ask. Leigh will rest her hand on my knee and I will look the three of them over. The three people I love most in the world.

"My other nipple feels neglected," Leigh says when we come up for air. "And this too." She takes my hand and guides it between her legs. I know what to do.

———

Our goodbye a few hours later is fraught with emotion. Leigh keeps glaring at me, giving the impression she can't quite believe the night we just had. I have trouble processing it myself, but I need to drag myself out of my current mindset, ignore the sting of my ass cheeks and focus on packing.

"Here." Leigh hands me her belt. "Something to remember me by." Before she releases it, she lets the leather slide through her fingers suggestively. Having it presented to me now makes me think back to yesterday's tears—mine, but especially hers. What is going on behind those eyes of hers?

"I won't forget you that easily." It was hard enough the first time.

Leigh's only half-dressed, but the clock is ticking and I need to see my son at breakfast. I no longer feel the need to admonish him, though it feels odd to have him involved in this. She comes for me and grabs me by the neck again.

"I've never forgotten you," she breathes into my ear, and I know it's true. Perhaps some people can have several true loves throughout their lives, but for me, there's only been one. It's her. I can't be sure what the future will bring, but I do know that, if we do get back together, it won't be a repeat of our previous relationship. There's no tuning back into old habits in the cards for us. I have an eight-year-old at home. And I'm a decade older, and hopefully wiser.

I check the clock again. "I have to go, Leigh." Instead of pulling away, I let her kiss me, and the touch of our lips swoops through me the way it has always done.

"Say hi to Troy for me." She chuckles and grabs the rest of her clothes. "And call me when you're back in New York." Her gaze lingers, waiting for a confirmation.

"I will."

One last quick kiss and I'm out the door. Part of me hopes she'll wait until I return to fetch my luggage after breakfast.

When he sees me approach his and Gerald's table Troy rises and opens his arms wide. I can't wait for him to be back in New York. To spend some proper time with him.

"I'm so sorry about last night, Mom." He pulls me into a tight, forceful hug. When did my little boy get so tall and strong?

"Sure you are." I sit across from him and examine his grinning face before saying hello to Gerald. "How was the game?"

"Do you really care?" Troy asks, still with a smirk on his face.

"Just checking if ditching your mother was worth it, Troy-toy." I send him a knowing smile back.

"How was your evening?" Gerald asks.

The chair feels extra hard against my bruised butt cheeks. "Interesting," I say. I don't want to quiz Troy in front of Gerald.

"I'm sorry about that, too, Mom." Troy is just a barrel of apologies this morning, though he doesn't come across as very repentant. "I know I should have told you much sooner that Leigh and I were friends. I just… never found the right time to tell you."

Friends? "I agree." I'm not letting him off the hook for keeping that a secret from me. "You should have said something." A waitress comes by and pours me a cup of coffee. "Especially because you've become quite… close."

"I know." He nods solemnly and I can so easily see he's not telling me everything.

"So how is Miss Sterling these days?" Gerald asks.

I wonder if she's still in my hotel room—the one my ex-husband so generously paid for. "Doing quite well for herself."

"How wonderful." He can't hide the sarcasm in his voice, not that I expect him to. Gerald has always been courteous with Leigh and any animosity between them always seemed to come more from her side. As though she couldn't stand the fact that I'd once been Mrs. Dunn. As though that had left a permanent stain on me—one even she couldn't erase.

"Let's order some food, shall we?" I say, diplomatically. Although I'm not hungry. My stomach is too aflutter with memories of Leigh. And exciting possibilities for our future.

CHAPTER TWENTY-THREE

I take Friday afternoon off in order to arrive in New York at a decent time. I don't want to knock on Jodie's door after midnight. Over the phone, I expressed my doubts about staying with her. What would she tell Rosie? Would I sleep on the couch? But Jodie told me not to worry about Rosie just yet. She'd sleep over at Muriel's and we could all meet for brunch on Saturday. Brunch with Muriel, I thought. What a delightful prospect. But only for a fleeting second because my mind was too hung up on Jodie and having the apartment to ourselves on Friday evening.

When I finally ring her bell an hour later than expected courtesy of 'mechanical issues' with the airplane, I'm so amped up, so ready to have her melt in my arms, I'm unprepared for the shock of just standing there. Of waiting for her to open the door for me in the building where I used to live—where, undoubtedly, throughout my life, I have been the happiest.

"Hey stranger," she says when she does open the door. Everything is treacherously familiar, but it's also not. The walls are a different color, and the sofa is in a different corner. Toys spill out of a box next to the kitchen door, and a large half-finished puzzle is spread out on the floor next to it. "Come in."

I drop my bag and take Jodie in my arms. I'm grateful to be able to close my eyes for a few seconds, and while I do so, I consider that arriving here, after all these years, feels much more like coming home than stumbling into my own house in San Francisco after a long day at work.

As I head out of the hallway I spot a picture of me and Troy in front of a huge Lego construction. I feel strangely honored that a minor souvenir of me has remained in Jodie's home.

"God, it's odd to be back here." I unbutton my blazer and glance around. She has a new sofa and a new dining table. I scan the walls for pictures of a person who might be Suzy, but can't immediately identify one.

"Drink?" Jodie has a silly grin plastered on her face.

"Oh yes." I sit down. The carpet is still the same one we had that bout of break-up sex on. I hope she had that cleaned.

"Do you still like a good red?" Jodie stands next to the drinks cabinet a few feet away from me. On the plane, I had visions of entering the apartment and slamming her against the door, the way I used to do, but the power of nostalgia seems to have me in its grip and I'm much more emotional than aroused right now.

I nod and look at Jodie. She has slipped into a pair of jeans —definitely after-work attire. Muriel and a good number of Jodie's colleagues used to wear jeans to work all the time but Jodie is not the type. She's wearing a baby blue blouse and whereas ten years ago it would have been tucked in tightly, she wears it loose now. But we've seen each other naked. I've let my eyes wander over the most-hidden parts of her body, and I know the score.

Jodie pours the wine. "A gift from Dan Mazlowski if you can believe it. Remember your old colleague?" She hands me the bottle, as though I need to read the label before I can drink it. "He's made quite a career for himself."

"I'm sure he has." Uninterested in the origin of the wine, I put the bottle down and raise my glass. "I guess we should drink to Troy," I say, my voice a bit hesitant, "for bringing us back together."

Jodie shakes her head. "He's sticking to his story that it was not a set-up."

"That boy will make a great lawyer very soon." I clink the rim of my glass against Jodie's and look her in the eyes. In all our time apart, I've never encountered irises as green as hers.

We fall silent and sip. The thought flits through my mind that the feelings we had for each other in Berkeley might have just been intensified melancholia. That the feeling might be unreproducible now that we're sitting here, in the same room where the disagreements started. That the magic might be gone. And we can't just fuck again. I want to ask about Jodie's exes—I've never been good at dealing with those—but right now is not opportune timing. Of all the things I had imagined I'd be doing right now, searching for words was not one of them.

"I told Muriel about, erm, our night in Berkeley." Jodie eyes me over the rim of her glass.

"Good old Muriel." Did she ever tell Jodie I ran into her not long after we broke up? And that she advised me to make contact? "What did she have to say?" Nerves tumble down my stomach. It still feels like most subjects should be carefully danced around.

"She gave me an eye-roll or two." Jodie chuckles. "You know what she's like."

"Look…" I feel agitated like a teenager on her first date. Insecure. "I've been thinking about moving back to New York for a while." I just blurt out the words. I haven't particularly spent more time considering coming back of late than at any other time over the years I went West. I also realize this is the wrong thing to say at this time. I just hope Jodie can see that I'm ill at ease. And that I'm sorry.

"Oh." She drinks, shifting uneasily in her seat. An image pops into my head of how she would look with her back against the wall and the button of her jeans flipped open. I'm all over the place. I have no idea what to say to Jodie Whitehouse. Being here is undoing me.

"I shouldn't have said that." I try a smile.

"I'm glad Troy did what he did," Jodie says, her gaze on me. "I'm glad I saw you again, Leigh. And I felt it too. That pull. All those memories. It was a crazy night, but a few hours in bed together can hardly erase all that has happened." She sighs. "Granted, it would be easy to just fall into bed"—an image of Jodie with her wrists tied to the headboard drifts through my mind—"but, I don't know if that's such a good idea. Eleven years is a long time."

I nod but still don't know what to say, until it comes to me. The truth that has been building in my subconscious for over a decade. The truth I was always too afraid to face. "I should have stayed." I put my glass down. "In the back of my mind, you were always there, Jodie. Even when I was with another woman, I was always silently comparing. I mean, I had to leave the city to get over you… and still I didn't see. I should have stayed. I should have been there when you had Rosie. I should have been there for everything because now, I sit here, and I want you so much it's nearly paralyzing me, but there's this huge gap between us. Not just caused by the years we've spent apart, but by the completely different lives we've led. I should have done it for you, Jodie. Gotten over myself and the pursuit of my precious career." I can't hold back a tear from sliding down my cheek. It's just the one though, like a dramatic metaphor for all the years I've spent alone.

"I disagree."

A jolt of hurt makes my head spin. She might as well have punched me in the stomach.

"You've changed," Jodie continues. "I can easily see that. What happened between us has changed you. And it's easy to sit here and think it could have worked if you'd stayed, but we were so miserable by the end. I would never have wanted a child to grow up in that atmosphere." Jodie deposits her wine glass on the table as well. "But how many people get a second chance? I, for one, had never expected you to sit in my apartment ever again. Our split hurt me so much, but I realize it was necessary. We wouldn't be who we are now if we hadn't broken up."

"Clearly you've been happier than I've been." Self-pity doesn't really suit me, so I straighten my spine and attempt a grin.

"I had a child, Leigh." She shuffles closer. "Here's my proposition." Her thigh is nearly touching mine. "Let's look to the future instead of at the past. What happened did so for a reason."

"Yeah." In response, I inch closer to Jodie. I'm not sure how serious she was about not falling into bed. My entire week has been consumed with images of her under my control. Of her bottom striped pink by my hand.

"I'm glad you came all this way." Jodie leans her head against my shoulder. "It feels like I missed you more during this week than I did the past eleven years combined."

Warmth spreads in my belly, and not just because of her touch. I brush her hair away from her ear so she can clearly hear what I'm about to say. "I want to fuck you." Because, before we can calm down and really assess this situation, I will need to possess her many more times. I will need to see her face scrunch up with ecstasy and hear her voice grow hoarse with pleasure.

"Okay," Jodie says, as if she, too, feels that we need to fuck this tension between us out of our system. As if it's the only way. It probably is. But it feels wrong to order her to go into the bedroom because it's not my bedroom anymore. She's slept with other people in that bed. Or perhaps, those ghosts need to be exorcized as well. It doesn't take me as long to find my bearings as it did in Berkeley when I was still too stunned by the shock of seeing her. First fully clothed, then naked, then with her hands tied to the bed.

I tune back into the fantasy that has dominated my nights—and days—since last weekend. "I brought something." Jodie slips off me when I get up. I head toward my bag and grab it. "Wait for me in the bedroom. Get naked. I need to use the bathroom."

Then I see it, what I've been waiting for since I arrived. That spark in her eyes. That upturned corner of her mouth. She's so beautiful, and so Jodie—every inch the woman from my memories. I can't wait to look into those eyes when I fuck her.

Silently, Jodie goes into the bedroom and leaves the door open. I enter the bathroom and peer at my reflection for a second. I'm back, I think, and for an instant, it feels as if I never left. Then I quickly disrobe and strap on. I paid a visit to my favorite shop in the Castro last Wednesday and picked this one out especially for our New York reunion. Just the feel of the dildo, as I maneuver it through the ring with my hands, leaves me weak at the knees.

Jodie's eyes widen when I walk into the bedroom. Then her lips stretch into a grin. "On your knees," I say. "Here." I point to the spot right in front of where I'm standing. "Now."

Jodie hurries off the bed and kneels before me. "You'd better make it nice and wet because I didn't bring any lube." I did, of course, but she doesn't have to know that. In my fantasy,

I added, "And I'll be damned if I'm going to use any of the stuff Suzy used on you," but I decide against that particular line. It's not necessary. Jodie's open mouth is hovering over the tip of my silicone cock already. "Eyes on me."

I didn't pick the smallest model, and that's an understatement. Jodie has to strain to wrap her lips around it and keep looking at me at the same time. I give her some time to find a rhythm and to get used to the action, but not too much, before grabbing a fistful of her hair and giving it a good tug. I yank at it until she stops. "You can do better." Her eyes are coated in tears already. She must be severely out of practice. When she sucks the dildo between her lips next, I give a little thrust, just to let her know I mean business. "Deeper," I growl. And she lets it slide further into her mouth until her eyes are bulging, and the sight unhinges something inside of me. No one has done this for me in such a long time. Her eyelids flicker open and shut as she works on my cock, until I say, "Enough." She lets it slip from her lips. Her mascara is smudged, a look I've always loved on Jodie. I give her a second to catch her breath.

"On the bed on all fours." I need to spend some time with her ass first. This was not part of my fantasy scenario either, but I can't help myself.

I wait until she's in position and then crawl behind her and let the dildo dangle between her legs. It's shiny with her spit and I need to stop myself from shoving it into her there and then, but that would just be giving her what she wants, and I do have some restraint left. I slither it against her pussy lips, let the tip graze against her clit, before pointing it at her ass cheeks and smearing them with saliva and her own wetness. My finger follows the dildo, meeting her flesh, and my own clit swells against the fabric of the harness. I could quite possibly come while fucking her. I spread her cheeks, just because I can, and because the sight never fails to arouse me, just to give the impression I'll be fucking her ass. I want to, but I want to look into her eyes more. I knead her ass cheeks, my fingertips leaving marks, and then let my fingers wander down to her cunt. I spread her lips and gather moisture. I just brought the lube as a precaution—because after so many years you just never know—but Jodie is sufficiently wet. I transport some of her juices to the dildo and rub it in my hand, lubricating it for entrance.

"Turn around," I hiss. I move to the side so Jodie can flip onto her back. "Legs wide."

Her teeth sink into her bottom lip. Whatever anyone else has done to Jodie in this bed and in this room, I'm ready to make it disappear. I'm ready to fuck the Suzy out of her—although I hardly think that's still necessary. It's more for me than for her. And even more than earlier, I feel as though I'm coming home.

I maneuver in between her legs and guide the cock to her glistening pussy lips. It has always astounded me how wet Jodie can get for me. My clit thumps against the panel of the harness. I need to fuck her as much for myself as for her.

"I'm going to fuck you so hard," I say, and Jodie drives her teeth further into her lips. She'll draw blood if she keeps this up.

By instinct, I guess, she brings her hands behind her head and holds on to the railing, but this is no time for restraints. This is us fucking in our old bed. I need her hands on me for that.

I push the tip in, eager to thrust, but, although I know full well how much Jodie can take, I give her some time to adjust first. I don't know how long it has been since someone fucked her with a strap-on. I do know it's been years since I felt the straps of a harness slice into my flesh, and that all that I have missed is bubbling to the surface in rapid, hot bursts.

I look at her pussy as I splay it open with my cock, then cast my eyes to her face. Jodie's mouth is open, her eyes narrowed. With one swift thrust, I'm deep inside of her and she gasps for air.

I lower my torso over her and plant my palms either side of her head. This is what I dreamed of. Me fucking Jodie while looking into her eyes. It's everything I hoped it would be. Plus, with every stroke inside of her, with every forward movement of my pelvis, my clit grazes against the inner panel of the harness. At first, I'm not entirely sure I want to lose control like that—and I wouldn't allow myself to with anyone else but her. But this is Jodie and I can tell she's getting aroused by the groans coming from my mouth. She releases the bed post and brings her hands to my shoulders, her nails digging in.

"Oh yes," she says. "Oh yes, Leigh." I fuck her harder, and by now my wetness must be overflowing from the harness, must be mingling with hers when I thrust, and the thought of our bodies meeting like that, and the realization that this is actually happening—that I'm fucking Jodie in her bed in her apartment in New York—spurs me on. I give her long, deep strokes and when she lets her head fall back I demand she look at me, and she does, and when her eyelids flutter open, and the green of her eyes shines through a film of tears, I let go. I come while inside her, and I can barely keep my own eyes open for it. I force them open, however, because I want to see.

"Come for me," I ask, although, admittedly, it sounds more like begging in that moment. An aftershock runs through me, throws me off-rhythm, but this is Jodie beneath me, and I know she hasn't changed that much that she can't come for me anymore when I ask. I see the orgasm ripple through her, her muscles shuddering, her mouth widening, her nails leaving marks.

"Oh fuck," she moans. And I look into her eyes, green slits in her face.

I stay inside of her a few more seconds before slowly retreating.

The harness and dildo are a nuisance now and I want to get them off me, but not as much as I want to kiss Jodie. So the silicone is sandwiched between us as I press my body to hers and kiss her for the first time today.

CHAPTER TWENTY-FOUR

It's a useless ride really—except for romantic purposes—but Rosie said she didn't mind the trip to the airport, so we see Leigh off together on Sunday evening. Rosie ended up staying at Muriel and Francine's for two nights in a row.

"Does that make me a bad mother?" I asked Leigh, who really was not the right person to ask.

"Nothing will ever make you a bad mother." She said the right thing but spanked me harder afterward nonetheless.

The three of us sit squeezed in the back of a taxi, Rosie half on my lap, Leigh's shoulder pressed into mine. I can't explain what she does to me, but maybe I needed a break from that intense longing in order to have another child. In hindsight, there were many justifications for our break-up. As many as there are now reasons to try again. Because, en route to JFK, it hits me again that the failure of my affairs with Amy and Suzy was all down to me. It wasn't so much that they couldn't give me what I craved in the bedroom, but what Leigh did give me. What she's given me now. And after a weekend of almost nothing but fucking, she still leaves me wanting more.

"When can I go on a plane again, Mommy?" Rosie asks.

Leigh nudges her in the arm and takes on a conspiratorial tone. "I'll work something out with your Mom, Rosie. I think both of you should come and see me soon."

I have to stop myself from suggesting next weekend. I would even let her pay for it. But we are not hormonal teenagers. We are women in our forties with responsibilities and full lives—and my parents are coming to New York next weekend.

"Do you want to take this slow?" Leigh asked me in bed this morning.

"You're the one who suggested moving back to New York as soon as you set foot in my apartment on Friday." I smiled at her, indicating it was a joke, but it felt like a lesbian cliché nevertheless.

"Touché," she said while searching for my nipple with her fingers. "Forgive a smitten girl for being nervous."

"'Smitten' I can live with." I caught her fingers with mine and brought them to my mouth. "'Girl' is stretching it a bit far." I sucked her fingers deep into my mouth and conversation was stopped again.

Now I'm about to say goodbye to Leigh, to watch her plane fly off, with nothing but a Skype date to head home with, and no clear idea of when we'll see each other again. Although until last weekend, I hadn't seen her for eleven years, this separation now seems cruel and harder to deal with. Once more, in a moment of despair, I find myself holding on to my daughter. The awkwardness of kissing Leigh goodbye in front of Rosie doesn't stack up against the pure need coursing through me to feel her body press against mine one last time before she goes.

"I love you," Leigh unexpectedly whispers in my ear, after we break from the kiss, but still have our arms wrapped around each other. "Always have."

Her words connect with something deep inside of me, maybe my soul, maybe the nostalgia of all the memories that have come flooding back, or maybe the part of me that's been missing since we broke up. "I love you too," I hear myself say, becoming more of a cliché as the seconds tick by. But it comes from the bottom of my heart.

Leigh folds her long body and crouches by Rosie's side. I had intended for them to spend more time together. I really wanted her to get to know Rosie—to, perhaps, show Leigh that the pain we suffered through was for the best reason imaginable.

"It was very nice to meet you, Rosie," she says, and seeing them together like that is almost too much. Tears well in my throat, but when you become a mother you learn to swallow your own tears in favor of your child's, and I try to apply that technique, but it doesn't seem to work when Leigh is standing next to me. "I will see you again very soon."

Rosie folds her little arms around Leigh's neck as far as they will go, and Leigh's face peeks through Rosie's curls, and I see her eyes are moist, too.

"She's a very affectionate child," Leigh says after she's stood back up.

"She's a hugger, all right. She'd hug the taxi driver if I let her." I smile down at my little girl. What would have happened if she hadn't had the flu last week? Would everything have been different? Would we all be standing here saying goodbye?

"I'd better go." Leigh blows Rosie and me one last kiss. I watch her make her way to security, and this seems to take too long for Rosie because she's already tugging at my sleeve.

"Don't be sad, Mommy," she says. "Leigh said she'd see us both soon." To her, all words are still the truth. But, when it comes down to these words, I do know that they are.

"So you're getting back together with her?" Muriel asks. I'm not feeling like work this Monday morning, and we've ditched it for half an hour to get a coffee at the Starbucks around the corner from our office.

Yes, I want to scream, but I don't want to offend Muriel's natural—and logical—skepticism too much.

"Just like that?"

"Not 'just like that'…"

"How then?" Muriel enjoys playing devil's advocate.

"For starters, it will have to be long distance for a while…"

She doesn't let up. "For a while? Have you booked the U-Haul already?"

I shake my head at her obvious comment. "Why are you giving me such a hard time about this? It's hard enough as it is already."

"Just making sure your head's still screwed on the right way, girl."

I gaze into my coffee dreamily. "I know this sounds foolish, but it's as if I know for a fact that she will never hurt me again…" I can't help but chuckle. "Well, not emotionally, anyway."

It's Muriel's turn to shake her head. She throws in an eye-roll as well. "You're my best friend, Jodie Whitehouse, and I consider myself an open-minded woman, but that part I never really understood."

"There's no need for you to understand." I go all warm inside at the memory of Leigh entering my bedroom fully strapped on. Not of the first time, but on Saturday night, when she fucked my ass with it.

Muriel gives me a judgmental 'uh-huh', but I know she's not judging, just playing. Apart from Leigh, she probably knows me the best.

"Well, I have some news as well." She taps her fingers on the table. "This weekend I plan to ask Francine to finally make an honest woman out of me. Got her a fancy-ass ring and everything."

"Oh." I've always admired Muriel and Francine's relationship, but in any other circumstances I wouldn't go all mushy about this. I do today. "That's just…" I choke up.

"I was going to ask you to be my maid of honor but if you're going to cry about it, I may need to revise my choice." Muriel shoots me a big smirk.

"I'm just really happy for you." And for myself, I think. The sniveling doesn't seem to stop. I barely shed a tear after I broke up with Amy and Suzy, but the rivers I cried after Leigh must still be fresh on Muriel's mind as well.

"You have a strange way of showing it." Muriel shuffles her chair a little closer. "The way you're bawling now, it makes me wonder if you've been secretly infatuated with Francine for years."

I chuckle through my tears. "Not with Francine," I say.

"I know." Muriel throws an arm around me. "Now stop ruining my blissful moment of announcement with your emotional fragility." She squeezes my shoulder.

"I mean it," I say. "I'm so happy for you." And for me, I think, even though it feels like such easily breakable, flimsy happiness.

"Don't be happy for me yet. She still has to say yes." Muriel is patting my biceps now.

"True." I manage to pull myself together a bit. "Do keep me posted on that." I can finally smile at my friend. It's not my habit to fall apart like this.

"Can you spank someone via Skype?" Muriel asks. "'Cause if you can, just have her do that. I'm sure it will make you feel better."

I spend the rest of the day as an overly emotional but ridiculously happy wreck.

CHAPTER TWENTY-FIVE

"You seem so much more relaxed these days." I've taken an entire week off to spend with Jodie in New York. Steve could hardly argue because since I moved West in 2003 I must have accumulated a few months' worth of vacation days.

"I'm much older now," Jodie says. We're sitting on the exact same bench we used to sit on when we took Troy to the park. "And everything is different."

"That pile of dishes in the sink is probably what threw me the most."

"I'm sorry. I really wanted the place to be spotless for you." For a second, Jodie looks genuinely concerned. "But my night scrubbing days are over."

"Who would have thought?" I nudge her with my knee.

"Who would have thought you and I would be sitting on this bench again one day?" Jodie looks happy. Because of the physical distance between us, and because Skype sex is not my idea of a good time, she and I have had to talk much more than we would have done if we'd been in the same city. During our last call, I touched on the subject of moving back to New York —a subject I'm keen to pick back up today.

"I tried to call you one night from San Francisco," I blurt out in response. "Karen had just broken up with me because I was being a shitty girlfriend and I thought, fuck it, I'm calling Jodie. It went straight to voicemail, though, but I sometimes wonder what would have happened if you'd picked up. If we'd been ready."

"We'll never know." Jodie has her eyes trained on Rosie, who's playing with some other kids on the swings. "But I'm fairly certain you and I could never have just been friends. We were never meant to be friends. Amy and Suzy are exes I could be friends with, but you… never."

"Gee, thanks," I joke.

"Not that I'll ever be friends with Amy. I don't blame her for holding a grudge. I was a pretty shitty girlfriend myself."

"Speaking of being girlfriends…" Even though I know the answer to my question because it can't be more obvious, nerves rattle me. "Are we… girlfriends again?"

Jodie chuckles. "We are women in our forties, Leigh. I hardly think the term 'girlfriends' applies." She averts her gaze from the playground and looks at me. "How many times have we fucked since Berkeley?" She pretends to count in her head, then nods. "Yes, I think we can call that going steady." She breaks out into a crooked, purple-lipped Jodie-smile.

"Can we just pick things up again, though, Jodes?"

"Just pick things up?" She shakes her head. "Eleven years have passed. So, no, of course, we can't. But… I think that… I can only be truly happy with you."

"It's funny, but Troy actually said something of the sorts to me about you a while back."

"I guess he knows his mother well." The smile fades from Jodie's lips. "And he was always extremely fond of you."

"I've made many mistakes in my life, Jodie."

"You've changed a lot," Jodie says. "Are you the same person who always claimed that motherhood was not in her blood?"

"I am and I'm not," I say. "But, yes, I guess people do change."

"But so fundamentally?" Jodie urges. "To change your mind on such a big issue?"

"I didn't change my mind, Jodes." I shift position, straightening my spine. "Life did." I gaze into Jodie's green eyes. "Life without you." I pause. These words are of the utmost importance. "And how hard it hit me when Troy emailed me." I look away briefly. "I suffered after our break-up but I buried myself in work and found other means to forget. But it wasn't until I met up with Troy that first time that I realized how much pain I had caused everyone—myself included. I'd always so firmly believed I was saving us and, regardless of us needing to spend time apart, and everything happening for a reason, when I saw him again, something clicked. Something I hadn't allowed to compute in my brain for a long time." I steady my gaze on Jodie again. "I nearly broke down in front of him. After he showed me a picture of Rosie and I realized that what I had been so afraid of, what I had been so convinced of not wanting, was a smiling little girl." I shake my head. "Perhaps things would have been different if I'd met someone else, but only now can I see that I was never even open to the option. Your memory was always lurking in the background. It has always been you, Jodie." Tears have been brimming since I began this impromptu speech and they are now close to breaking.

Jodie shuffles a little closer.

"There are many rational reasons for the years we spent apart. I guess the most convincing one is that I wasn't ready. That I couldn't see past my own goals to meet yours until after I'd gone eleven years without you. And it's true that I've always believed that I wasn't a mother, that I just didn't have it in me. Not the desire, nor the necessary skills—or time for that matter. But then I look back at what Troy and I had, and my persistence in not wanting to be called Mom or even feeling like his mother, but, actually, I was doing everything a mother did. I did have his best interests at heart. I attended his soccer games. I attempted to make him an edible dinner once in a while." I try a shy smile. "I sat up with him when he was ill. I worried about him after dark. I wondered about his future."

"Okay," Jodie says and gives me one of those smiles that drive me wild. "It was very obvious you weren't ready for the things I wanted. Even though 'ready' is probably not even the right word."

Rosie comes running toward us. Her eyes twinkle and her curls bounce around her head. She has the same eyes as Jodie and Troy.

"Thirsty?" Jodie asks.

Rosie nods and Jodie produces a juice carton from her bag. Rosie tips her head back and drinks it with both hands clasped around the carton. Once it's empty, Rosie wants to give it back to Jodie, who refuses to take it.

"You know what to do with that."

Rosie gives her a quick pout, struts to the garbage can on the edge of the playground, and then rejoins her friends.

"She's so adorable." It's more thinking out loud than engaging in conversation.

"You used to say that about Troy when we came here with him." Jodie's tone isn't resentful.

"I know. He *was*."

"Do you want to come live with Rosie and me?" Jodie turns toward me.

"I'm certainly moving back to New York. I've worked my butt off for that firm the past decade. I don't think anyone can refuse me the request." I stretch my arm along the back of the bench, finding Jodie's neck with my fingers. "Do you really want me to move in straight away?"

"Why not?" Jodie's eyebrows twitch. "I *know*, Leigh. I know here." She taps her chest dramatically. "I know that we belong together. Why waste any more time?" She shuffles backward, leaning into the grasp of my fingers. "It's so obvious to me now. When Amy asked me to move in with her, all I had were doubts. With Suzy…" She pauses. Suzy, whom I'm bound to meet once I move back, whom Rosie calls 'Auntie Suzy'. "Even with Suzy it wasn't the same. Not by a long shot. I've never known the way I do when I'm with you."

"You've grown more sentimental with age as well." I squeeze Jodie's neck between my fingers.

"So what? There's something to be said for becoming a sentimental fool."

"Back to York Avenue…" Some serious down-sizing will be in order, but I don't want to break the magic of the moment. Has anything been done to the place at all since I left?

"I know it's cramped, but we'll figure something out." Jodie puts a hand on my thigh. Her touch makes me melt.

"I'll start packing as soon as I get back." And put my house on the market, I think.

"I predict we'll be sitting on this very bench twenty years from now. Troy might have children by then. We can take our grandkids to the park."

It's the 'our' that almost makes me well up.

CHAPTER TWENTY-SIX

Leigh is flying back to San Francisco tomorrow and I can't sleep. It's still the same alarm clock that sheds its faint red light into my room—these objects, if treated right, are indestructible. It makes me think of the sleepless nights I spent here on my own over the years. The weeks of agony before breaking up with Amy, during those nights that she believed I should have spent with her in Brooklyn. The long, frantic dawns worrying about what to do about Suzy, whose presence in my apartment—and my life—seemed to be getting bigger and bigger. Too big for my comfort.

But, mostly, I reminisce about the nights I tossed and turned while missing Leigh. She's a wide sleeper, who likes to stretch her arms and legs, claiming her territory—funny how she's even like that when sleeping. From what she's told me, for the past eleven years, she has mostly slept alone, not having encountered many reasons to improve her sleep etiquette. I'll need to get used to having her in my bed again. In *our* bed.

Even though I can't sleep, it feels right. Leigh and I spent many a sleepless night in this bed together as well. She stayed up with me when Troy was sick and his fever worried me. She sat by my side until the morning light broke when a boy whose case I was responsible for committed suicide and I nearly went to pieces with grief and frustration.

One night, when we'd been together for about a year, we remained awake all night, giddy with excitement, dreaming up our future. Leigh would say silly things like, "I'll become D.A. and you can be my trophy wife" or "we'll move into a penthouse on Park Avenue." I would tickle her until she took the trophy wife remark back. I ignored the Park Avenue comment.

Sometimes, just before falling asleep, she would say something along the lines of, "Are you sure you locked the door, Jodes?" Just to tease me, because she knew all too well I would need to get up and check. Afterward, she'd make sure I was exhausted enough to go to sleep right away once she was done with me.

Now, she seems to breathe heavier than she used to. A light purr comes from her side of the bed—which is also half my side. Just after we broke up, I was convinced that as soon as Leigh moved to the other coast, some lucky woman without any desire for children would snap her up and never let her go. How could that not happen? Turns out Leigh didn't allow herself to be snapped up. The other day she said that, for her, the years we spent apart could be easily summed up in one word: lonely.

She turns on her back and shoves her hand into my shoulder in the process. Maybe in a few years a gesture like that will irritate the hell out of me, but now, on the cusp of our second life together, it only makes me smile. I take her hand in mine. I don't want to spend our last night together asleep. I start stroking her palm, realizing that we are too old to pull an all-nighter, but I don't care. I want to look into her big brown eyes. I want to make plans for our future again. Real plans.

"Can't sleep?" she says when she opens her eyes.

"It's not easy with someone like you in my bed." I give her a mock sigh.

"Because I'm too sexy?" Her lips curve into a crooked grin. Her cheeks are slack with the remnants of sleep. She looks so relaxed, so completely where she needs to be.

"Because you take up too much room."

"Would you like me to sleep on the sofa?" Her hand is stroking my belly, but she knows I don't want to do what she's thinking of because of Rosie sleeping in the other room. Not an issue I ever had with Suzy—because Suzy never made me scream the way Leigh does.

I curve my arm around her back to let her know she's not going anywhere until she has to leave for the airport tomorrow.

"Remember when you lay here with me one night and you proclaimed you'd become D.A. one day?"

"I said that? No way." Her hand keeps flitting along the sensitive skin of my belly and my C-section scar.

"That was before you got dollar signs in your eyes and joined Schmidt & Burke. When I still believed you were idealistic like me." I let a finger skate along her cheek.

"I was never idealistic like you. Never to the same degree, anyway."

"Perhaps we would never have met if you hadn't worked for the D.A.'s office. Or I would have been put off by your criminal defense lawyer ways if we'd met later."

"Too many 'ifs' for this hour of the night, Jodie."

"What happened to the Leigh who could stay up until morning and dream with me?" My finger has reached her hair. I've spotted some gray ones above her ears, but I haven't told her yet.

"She's tired." In the semi-darkness, I see Leigh's eyes sparkle nonetheless. "But I'll tell you this, just so you'll never forget." She inches a little closer. "You and I were destined to meet, I'm sure of it. And, no, I don't care if that sounds too sentimental for the sane people we consider ourselves to be. Only a few days ago, I believe, I heard someone talk about sentimentality and such." She chuckles. "A wise woman, I seem to remember, considering her age and so on."

I dig my fingertips into Leigh's scalp. "I guess it would be equally foolish to consider whether we're going too fast?"

Leigh pushes herself up a bit, her hand falling away from my belly in the process. She looks fully awake now. "It's not foolish at all, but, like you, I just… know. I know that I want to be here with you. Being anywhere else right now would make me more miserable than I've been in the past eleven years combined."

"I'm not having any seconds thoughts, either." I scoot closer and wait for her to kiss me.

"We should get some sleep though, Jodes," Leigh says after.

"Fine." I crash down and turn on my side, my back to her. "Spoon me, please. And don't fall asleep before I do."

Leigh folds her tall body around mine and whispers, "You know what happens when you're too bossy for your own good." She's asleep within minutes.

I still can't sleep, not even with Leigh's arm resting on me, with her breath in my ear. Or, perhaps because of it. The short conversation we just had about her becoming D.A. reminds me of the day she got hired at Schmidt & Burke.

"I solemnly swear to you, Jodie Whitehouse, that it will become Schmidt, Burke & Sterling within the next ten years," she'd proclaimed. By then, I had seen Leigh in various states of ecstasy, but never when her job was involved. Pure happiness seemed to radiate from her skin, and I absorbed it gladly. I wanted nothing more than for Leigh to be happy, for her to get everything she wanted in life. She'd had to go for several interviews before they finally offered her a contract, and I had supported her every step of the way.

I'd even considered it a privilege to see Leigh with her confidence frayed at the edges—she was never one to totally crack—and to see her fidget with her fingers uncontrollably, her eyes going all dark and serious.

"I hadn't pegged you for the nervously pacing type," I said, the night before her last interview. "It's in the bag already, surely. I'm certain all you'll need to do at this point is manage to hold a pen in your restless fingers long enough to sign on the dotted line."

"This is no joke, Jodes," she said in her formal court voice. "I've wanted this for a long time."

I guess I could see it then, on full display, how blind desire can make a person behave. How having eyes on the prize can chip away at their common sense.

Although Leigh had made it clear from the very beginning that she wouldn't be a career ADA, she had consulted me extensively before finding the law firm she wanted to join and getting to work on accomplishing that goal.

"You're an inextricable part of my life now, Jodie," she had said, "I need to know how you feel about this."

By then I had worked for the ACS for more than five years and I had seen many an excellent ADA join law firms. It always made me a little sad because it meant that the private sector would, once again, gain what the state was losing in experience. I didn't object, of course. If that was all it took to fulfill Leigh's deepest wishes, she could become the slickest lawyer she needed to be, put in the required hours to make her name partner ambitions clear, and attend after work drinks to suck up to people who were silly enough to need it. Leigh always had my support. Between the two of us, Gerald, a string of regular babysitters, and Muriel and Francine, we had Troy's wellbeing more than covered.

Most of that blind ambition has gone now. She got what she wanted—and life has changed her.

Carefully, I extract myself from her grasp and watch how she rolls onto her back. I'm ready to start again with this new, mature, wiser version of Leigh Sterling.

CHAPTER TWENTY-SEVEN

"Your house is so big, but you hardly have any stuff," Jodie says.

"I've gotten rid of a lot of things already." It strikes me that I brought zero lovers to this place. I invited one woman back once, but I had to ask her to leave before we could actually become lovers because I'd totally misread her and she tried to shove *me* against the wall.

"All the sex toys you used with other women, you mean?" Jodie stands by the window, looking out. The things I want to do to her in this house.

"I told you. I had one semi-serious relationship and I screwed that one up as well."

"Was she"—Jodie turns around, curling her fingers around the edge of the window sill—"kinky like me?"

Jodie seems to be suffering from the same affliction as me: irrational jealousy of ex-partners. "Oh yes," I tease because Karen might have been the right amount of kinky for me, but it was never the same as with Jodie.

"Did you... do things with her that you didn't do with me?"

She sinks her teeth into her bottom lip and that's how I know this is foreplay. So much for both being the jealous type.

I discard the box I'm filling and walk over to her. She's already positioned perfectly in front of the window. I stop a few feet away from her and look her in the eyes. "I did." It's not true, but it doesn't matter.

"Do it to me."

Blood rushes to my clit. Since our reunion, I've let Jodie fuck me a lot more times than when we were first together—as though I've been in a constant, unquenchable state of arousal. As though merely dominating Jodie isn't enough anymore.

"I let her tie me up and fuck me any way she wanted to," I say.

Jodie narrows her eyes. She doesn't believe me. That too doesn't matter. If I tell her to fuck me, she will.

"Any way she wanted to?" Her voice quivers.

I fold my arms over my chest. "Yes."

"With your hands tied up?"

I nod.

"Do... you want me to do that you?" Jodie understands that this would not be a matter of reversing roles, and that, throughout, I would be in full control.

"Yes." I keep my voice steady, but lust rages in my blood.

"Now?" Her fingers hold on to the ledge a bit tighter.

I nod again.

Jodie sucks her lip into her mouth. It turns me on more. I don't crave to have my hands immobilized, but I do want to see what tying me up would do to her. I want to see the look in her eyes when she loops a belt around my wrists.

"Come here," she says, and I bridge the gap between us.

Her hands go straight for my belt and when she unbuckles it, liquid lust pools between my legs. She tugs the belt from the loops of my jeans and inspects it. She might not have laid her eyes on it many times, but she sure has felt it crack against her ass on numerous occasions already. Last night, for instance, when she arrived at my house. She'd said she wanted to see it before I left for good and promptly booked a ticket to San Francisco. That particular belt and Jodie's behind became intimately acquainted all of last night. She barely got a chance to see the house.

She unbuttons my jeans next. "You do the rest," she instructs, in a voice more sure of itself than I had anticipated.

Methodically, I take off my clothes, and just to grate on her nerves a little, let them fall to the floor.

"Sit on the window sill with your arms stretched above your head." Jodie moves away from the window. It looks out over a bunch of backyard bushes and I know that, disappointingly, nobody will be able to see.

Once I've found my position, Jodie looks me over for a second, and I can see the excitement glitter in her glance. It matches the thrills chasing up my own spine. I hike my knees up and spread wide for her without her having to ask—my own little triumph at this moment.

She proceeds to fasten my wrists to the handle of the window. They're not tied very securely, but it's the thought that matters most. Jodie has never seen me like this. I've never been in this position. The newness of the situation sets something off in my blood, and I need to swallow the words 'fuck me now' because they have no place in this scenario.

Jodie hoists her t-shirt over her head and stands before me in her bra and jeans. My clit stands to attention more. My nipples are so hard they almost hurt.

"Let's see how many fingers Leigh Sterling can take," Jodie says, and the way she pronounces the words, without a trace of doubt in their tone, makes my head spin. She doesn't bring her fingers to my pussy lips, though, but instead circles one around my clit—something I hardly ever do to her. "You'd better not come," she groans, and I can tell that, now that she's touching me, she has trouble controlling herself. How wet she must be. The prospect of touching her cunt later brings me another few seconds closer to climax. "Because I haven't fucked you yet." She keeps trailing her finger around my clit, and I make a mental note to commend her on her torture technique later, but right now, I need to wriggle my ass and hold on to something inside myself in order not to come at Jodie's finger.

"How many do you think, Leigh?" she asks. "Three? Four?" Her finger halts its motion. "All five?"

Admittedly, I have to swallow hard at these questions. It could be that I overplayed my hand. Speaking of hand… Jodie's hand is now lowering itself between my legs. Her fingers lightly skate over my drenched lips. I look down at her hand and my pussy, but I don't have a lot of room to maneuver so I can't make out how many fingers she's actually planning on fucking me with.

I don't reply to her question because I realize that the biggest thrill lies in leaving it up to her. How far will she go? Can she even do this? Jodie has fucked me before, of course, but never like this. And never with more than three fingers.

"Let's start with two and work our way up, shall we?" Jodie looks astoundingly gorgeous in the moment that she says it. The light illuminates her face and brings out the green in her eyes. And those lips that always go a bit crooked when she speaks. I wouldn't mind those on my clit later… Two fingers inside of me stop my thought process. Jodie is gentle, but with her other hand, she finds my breast and pinches my nipple.

I'm so aroused I could probably come after a few more strokes, but I know the rules of this game better than anyone.

Jodie increases the rhythm of her fingers and I wrap mine around the belt tightly. She doesn't say she's adding a third finger, but I certainly feel how she spreads me wider. She doesn't give me a lot of time to adjust, either, and amps up the speed with which she's fucking me again. I'm starting to unravel. It begins somewhere beneath my ribs and soon seizes my muscles.

"Jodie, I—" I can't take it anymore, I want to say, but the words die in my throat and the grin Jodie shoots me saturates my flesh with another bout of lust and the thrill of coming for her like this, hands tied, surprises me with its strength.

Jodie's fingers retreat and she holds two of them up to me. They're wet with my juices. "I lied," she says. "I only used two."

I burst out in giggles while she unties the belt. Once my arms are free I pull her toward me. "I'll have you for this."

"I was hoping you would." Jodie pushes herself back and glares at me.

"Very well." I hop off the window sill and tell her to take off her jeans and take my place.

I don't bother with tying her up. I only have eyes for what lies between her legs. Her pussy is soaked, her lips puffy and a deep red, her clit so swollen she'll probably come with just one flick of my tongue against it. And I can't help myself. I need to taste her. When I kneel in front of her, I think that not everything has to stay the same. We're not the same people anymore in so many more ways than I had first believed.

Jodie's hands are in my hair as I let my tongue touch down on her lips first, trailing between them, and then I feast on her clit. I suck it between my lips and flick my tongue against it while my nose inhales everything of her.

"Oh, Jesus." Jodie's fingers tug at my hair. Her heels dig into my shoulders.

I lick Jodie in a way that I hardly ever do: gentle, deliberate, not withholding anything. Soon her thighs are clasped against my ears and she expels a high-pitched roar.

When I push myself free from the grip of her thighs and look at her, she's snickering with her back pressed against the window.

"What?" I ask.

"That was certainly different." She hoists me toward her.

"Wouldn't want you to get bored." I'm still a little ambivalent about what just happened.

"Bored?" She presses a kiss onto my forehead. "Did you really let your ex fuck you like that?" There's insecurity in her voice.

"Of course not." My mouth is pushed against her shoulder.

"I knew that." She grabs me by the shoulders so she can look at my face. "I did."

I nod. We'll continue this conversation later—probably in a similar situation and without words. "If you want me all settled in before Muriel's engagement party, we'd better get a move on. I thought you came here to help me pack."

"Oh, I can pack as well if you want me to," Jodie says, a wide grin on her face.

"Don't push it." I fall back into her arms and kiss her.

As soon as I came back from that first weekend in New York with Jodie I started dropping hints at the office about moving back East.

"We could use your expertise to expand the Boston office," Steve said at first.

"No," I replied. "I'm needed in New York."

CHAPTER TWENTY-EIGHT

Rosie's a flower girl at Muriel and Francine's wedding. She walks down the aisle with the biggest look of concentration on her face.

Don't cry, don't cry, don't cry, I tell myself. She has experienced a growth spurt of late and I can't help but wonder if in a few years' time both my children will tower over me. Leigh sits on my right and Troy on my left. He's almost finished with his first year of Law in Boston, which is only a four-hour drive away so I get to see more of him.

With the money from the sale of her house in San Francisco Leigh bought a townhouse on the same street as Gerald.

"Imagine that," I said. "Next you'll be having dinner parties together."

"He's not too bad, I guess," Leigh said when we celebrated after we'd signed the deeds. I'd protested at first, of course. My financial independence, however difficult it has proved over the years, has always been a point of pride for me.

"Don't be so Irish, Jodie," Leigh said. "Your name needs to be on this title. It's the only sane thing to do." I knew she was right. If I was finally going to give up my apartment on York Avenue, I did want my name on the papers. "This is our house."

"What's with all the sniffling, babe," she whispers in my ear now. "Are you going through *the change?*" I know she's only saying that to make me laugh—and make me snap out of this emotional haze—but I've actually wondered the same thing lately.

"Shut up. I need to focus." But I well up again as I see first Muriel and then Francine strut toward the front. Muriel is beaming, a bright smile plastered on her face, and she winks at me when she passes and turns to take her spot for the ceremony.

Leigh doesn't know what I have planned for after this wedding, which I should give my full attention. My best friend doesn't get married every day, after all.

"We're going to *Muriel's wedding*," Leigh has repeatedly said to Rosie over the past few days, but the joke was always completely lost on the girl. She has no interest in Australian movies from the early nineties. Leigh, on the other hand, convinced me to watch the film with her. We have a TV set in our bedroom now. What we watch most on it, when we have the house to ourselves, is a video Leigh made of me while I penetrate myself with a dildo for her. She says nothing has ever made her come as hard as fucking while that video is on.

I didn't realize until a few weeks ago that being a maid of honor is really only an honorary title. At least when it comes to this wedding.

"I don't want no attention on you," Muriel said when I asked her about my duties. "It's bad enough I have to share the bridal spotlight with Francine. Just organize me a bachelorette party and that'll be that."

I want nothing more than for everyone's gaze to be trained on the happy couple. Rosie's job is done and she rushes to my side. I put a hand on her shoulder. So does Leigh.

The wedding officiant says a few words about both of them and then proceeds to proclaim their union.

"Seriously?" I had asked Muriel when I went wedding gown shopping with her. "White?"

"What else am I going to wear? Red?"

"Cream or beige or that lilac one over there doesn't look half bad."

"Sometimes I wonder if you know me at all." She scrunched her lips into a defiant pout. "I'm having a white wedding." Muriel could never stay serious for very long. "Well, dress-wise at least."

Now, her dark skin contrasts heavily with the white of her dress. Francine looks dapper in a white suit with soft violet accents. If she wanted to wear any other color, I'm certain her wife-to-be set her straight—so to speak—soon enough.

"You have to cry at your own wedding," I said to her last night. "I mean, you won't be able to stop yourself."

"I'm sure you'll do all the crying for me," Muriel said in her typical Muriel way. "I'm from Harlem. We don't cry in Harlem."

"I'm from Connecticut, which is not exactly the state best known for its tear-shedding inhabitants either."

"Do you, Muriel Ilene Williams take Francine Watts to be your lawfully wedded wife?" the officiant asks.

"I do," Muriel says in a loud, booming voice, lest there's someone at the back whose hearing aid is not working. And I see it glitter in the corner of her eye. Or perhaps it's the way the light slants through the window to her right.

Francine says "I do" next, after which they exchange rings, carried by Francine's nephew, James, and the ceremony ends.

"Stay behind for a bit," I say to Leigh after she gets up. My children are in on this and I want them here for this moment. Having them present is important to me.

Rosie stands grinning beside Leigh. Troy, a real man now,

with a beard he refused to shave off even for this occasion, shifts his weight from one foot to the other nervously.

"What's going on?" Leigh asks. The place is emptying rapidly.

I feel for the box in my pocket and go down on one knee. Rosie's already squealing with delight.

"Leigh Sterling." I look up at her. "Will you marry me?"

Leigh glares at me, then shifts her gaze to Rosie and then to Troy. Her face breaks into a smile. "I can hardly say no in front of your children, can I?"

I feel the tears coming already. I won't be able to stop them now.

"Yes," she finally says. "A million times yes."

Rosie's jumping up and down. Troy is wringing his hands together. I wonder if he's holding back tears as well, or perhaps he's just embarrassed by his old Mom's antics. But, as far as I'm concerned, almost a year after his graduation from Berkeley, I wouldn't have just proposed to Leigh if it weren't for him.

Leigh pulls me up. "That's why you wanted to wear trousers?" She doesn't wait for a reply and throws her arms around me. Rosie hugs me from the side and from behind Leigh's back, Troy gives me a thumbs-up.

"I can't believe you still managed to steal my fucking thunder." Muriel does not look like a blushing bride. "You had the audacity to propose on my wedding day!"

"It… just seemed fitting," I stammer, gauging if she's actually mad—she certainly looks it—or if she's toying with me.

"You could have told me." Her hands are at her sides. "But fuck it, Jodie. Let's just make this party one big love fest." She pulls me into a hug that lasts much longer than our usual ones. "I'm glad you found each other again." When we let go, she peers at me. "I see now that no one else could ever be more perfect for you."

"Will you be my maid of honor, then?"

"Damn right I will be." She pulls her lips into a smirk. "And, no offense, but the bachelorette party I will throw you will not be as tame as that cocktail shaking class you set up." She nods as though very sure of something. "I'm taking you to Atlantic City."

The DJ changes the pace of the music to a slow song and I recognize the intro to "Show Me Heaven".

"For you," Muriel says. "So you can have a mushy dance with your fiancée."

I shoot Muriel a smile and, as I wander over to Leigh, I know that, if this had not happened, if Leigh and I had never seen each other again, my life would still have turned out sort of all right because I have a best friend like Muriel.

"May I have this dance?" I ask, bowing solemnly.

"You may." Out of habit, Leigh puts her hand on the small of my back as she guides me to the dance floor. I drape my arms around her neck and gaze up at her.

"Opening dance at our wedding, I presume?" Leigh quirks up her eyebrows.

"Everything is open to debate."

"Not everything." She slants herself toward me and kisses me lightly on the lips.

Troy wolf whistles at us. He's being a good sport and dancing with Rosie, who really should be in bed by now, but Muriel and Francine are her favorite aunts and her Mom just got engaged.

"How long have you known you were going to ask me today?"

I huff out an embarrassed chuckle. "I guess the idea first dawned on me when Muriel told me she was planning to propose to Francine."

"When was that?" Leigh cocks her head to the side.

"The Monday after you came back to New York for the first time." I push myself a bit closer toward her. "But it didn't… crystallize until a few months later," I say in my defense. "And hey, it beats blurting out that you want to move back to New York after just one night together."

"Fair enough." She leans her forehead against mine. "The real question, however, is how you managed to keep Rosie from telling me?" We both look at her dancing with Troy and she waves at us.

"Oh, I only told her three days ago. I knew from the start that would be a lost cause." We both wave back at Rosie. "I told Troy a few weeks ago when I went to see him in Boston. He finally admitted to arranging that basketball game excuse with his friend. There was a game, but he would never have gone if he had seen there was hostility between us. Then we would have ended up having dinner with him and Gerald."

Leigh shakes her head. "That boy."

Indeed, I think, that boy.

I sneak another peek at my children dancing together while Leigh pulls me closer to her, and the biggest rush of happiness moves through me.

CHAPTER TWENTY-NINE

It's hard to believe this is actually happening. It's an even further stretch that I agreed to have the wedding here, at Gerald's house in The Hamptons. But, perhaps, we had to come back and do it here—to right a wrong.

I'm rather notorious for my closing arguments in court, often speeches I slave over for hours, writing draft upon draft until they're perfect, but I haven't spent nearly as much time on any of them as I did on getting my vows right for this day.

It's a small group that has gathered here. Our parents. My brother Lex, forty and single. Perhaps he hasn't met his Jodie yet. I should tell him later that he shouldn't despair. Not that I think he does. Sonja. Steve and his third wife. Muriel and Francine. Ginny and Susan and their twins. Gerald and Elisa, whom I really think brings out a different, better side of Jodie's ex-husband. Rosie, of course, who's taking her role as only bridesmaid extremely seriously. And Troy, who, for the very first time, has brought a girl home. Her name is India, even though she's all American. She's studying computer sciences and looks like she spends too much time indoors, but she's sweet and Troy is very affectionate with her.

Jodie's reciting her vows first. She's gearing up for them now. I love her to bits, but I already know she won't make it through them without bursting into tears. She wasn't always like this. She claims to have changed in that department since she had Rosie. I also know that I'll need to read her vows on paper later to fully grasp them.

"Leigh," she starts. She's dressed quite informally for her own wedding. The Jodie I once knew would have been horrified at the idea of getting married in a linen pants suit. But here she stands. Her hair in the wind, eyes blazing. Those purple-painted lips—still the same lipstick—ready to pronounce the words.

After she asked me to marry her, it stung just the tiniest of bits because I had wanted to be the one who asked *her*. But I got over that by the time we left Muriel and Francine's wedding party.

"I decided to ask you to be my wife because, despite the years we spent apart, I've loved you all along. You once said to me that your passion for me eclipsed everything else, and I've always remembered that."

There we go. Her voice is ascending into a higher register already. I teased her about it last night, but she wouldn't have any of it.

"You'd better let me read them now because we both know you won't be able to say them tomorrow, babe," I said.

"I may surprise you," Jodie tried.

"Fine, but just a word of advice: keep it short. It's easier to cry through two or three sentences than through four pages of love declaration. I know how you feel about me already, anyway."

She didn't say anything, but I did notice later that she was huddled over a piece of paper and I might have heard some strike-through noises made by the tip of a pen.

It's not that Jodie's words don't matter to me. They do. But what we have between us is hard to put into words. We can try, but we both know we can't pour our feelings into a string of vows. We've been apart, and we know that's the last thing we want ever again. Nothing better to tie a couple together than an eleven-year separation.

"My passion for you..." The rest of Jodie's sentence gets swallowed by a sob. I can just make out 'equally' and then she goes silent. Our guests, who are standing around us in a casual set-up, shuffle around nervously a bit, but they're all familiar with Jodie so they know the deal.

"Oh, screw it," she stutters. "I love you, Leigh Sterling. I bloody well love you."

I squeeze her hand and look into her eyes. What does she see through her tears? The woman who left her or the woman who came back? I'm both, of course.

"Leigh," the officiant addresses me, "would you like to recite your vows?"

I most certainly do, I think, and clear my throat.

"Jodie." We decided long ago to not use traditional wedding vows, but to say something straight from the heart, and in our own words, instead. "This love, our love, is one that only comes along once in a lifetime." I curl my fingers around hers a little tighter. "When we met, everything changed. Because how could it not? Never in my life have I met someone more responsible, caring, sensual and with a heart so big it has room for all the foster kids in New York City." Damn, I'm starting to well up a bit too. But someone chuckled when I said 'sensual'— I bet it was Muriel—and it keeps my tears at bay.

"During the time we spent apart, no one even came close to you. No one." I grip her hand a bit tighter still. "Perhaps it's sad that I needed to be away from you, to be removed completely from your life, to see that there's only one woman on this planet for me. It would be ludicrous for me to stand here and to vow that I'll be forever faithful to you because there is not a person in this world who thrills me more than you do. And you know that when I say I only have eyes for you that I mean it." Regardless of my restraining efforts, the first tear slips out of my eye. "I don't believe it's possible to love another human being more than I love you. To fit together better with someone than how we fit together. To reach a level of happiness higher than what we've reached now. I love you, all of you. I love your family. Your children, Troy and Rosie. And I love all of us together."

Jodie is in tears. Perhaps it was a bit much. We still have to get through the 'I do's'. My own cheeks are hardly dry either. I want to give the officiant a hurry-up glare, but I can't keep my eyes off Jodie. The words I just spoke don't convey half of what I feel, but it was never words that tethered us to each other the most. It was only when we started using more words, and the arguments got heavier with them, that we started drifting apart.

The officiant finally proceeds. He must be used to this. All these emotions so blatantly on display. All this joy. I wonder what it does to a person. I hope he's not single.

During my years of loneliness in San Francisco, I never even considered marriage. Not just because it wasn't a legal option then, but because I was as far removed from the prospect as I could be. Now, though, not even a year after seeing Jodie again, I stand here and I say 'I do' with such pride in my voice, I believe it may just erase all the mistakes I made.

When our lips meet for the formal you-may-kiss-the-bride moment, I don't want to let go. Muriel never hesitates to inform us that her wedding night—as are most newlyweds' first nights together—was a big dud. She and Francine both crashed into bed exhausted from the day's events. I vowed to myself that this would not be the case for Jodie and me. It wouldn't suit us. Additionally, we have the hormonal advantage of our reacquaintance, with the accordingly high levels of arousal in our bloodstream.

When we finally break from the kiss, Jodie looks at the small group of people around us, and I follow her gaze. Rosie's smiling and crying at the same time. Troy and India are headed in our direction. So are our parents. It feels strange to be congratulated for my love for Jodie. She crouches down and picks up Rosie, who really is too big to be carried in her mother's arms, and a new rush of warm, all-encompassing love washes over me. I love that girl and there's nothing I wouldn't do for her. She knows it too and is already starting to take advantage of it.

"Come here." I hold out my hands to take Rosie from Jodie. She folds her arms around my neck and puts her head on my shoulder. No words are required. It reminds me of when she and Jodie waved me off at the airport that first time and she threw her little arms around me. What that impromptu hug told me was that everything would be different the second time around. And it has been. Jodie is my wife now. She put a ring on my finger. I know what the next step will be, but I haven't told her yet. First, we must celebrate.

The congratulatory part of the afternoon passes quickly. Jodie's not like Muriel in the sense that she didn't want to invite every distant acquaintance to our wedding.

"I don't want a big fanfare. I just want to be married to you," she said. "But it would be impolite to not at least invite our nearest and dearest."

When Gerald, an excellent neighbor and a surprisingly good cook for someone who works all the time, suggested his beach house as a venue, I guess it resonated with both Jodie and me. As though the only way to come full circle was to hold the ceremony here.

"Are you sure?" Jodie asked, after we'd already agreed.

"I do have one concern," I said. "You've taken your exes there. It might be awkward, what with the memory of them."

"Don't worry about that. I've forgotten all about them." It was just a manner of speaking, of course, because Jodie stayed friendly with Suzy for Rosie's sake. Apparently, Suzy was able to do that—I suppose I admire her a tiny bit for that. I've met her and I guess I can see what drew Jodie to her. But, to my utmost relief, she hasn't become that close a friend that Jodie invited her to our wedding.

Champagne flows freely well into the night. Most of the guests have booked accommodation in the area. This includes Gerald, who gallantly claimed that his house was ours for as long as we needed it. I also presume he didn't want to stay here on his ex-wife's wedding night.

"How strange," Jodie said, when we arrived here this morning, "that Gerald and I have grown closer since you arrived back into the picture. Who would have thought?"

"Life is strange," I replied enigmatically. And it is.

Jodie's just freed herself from a conversation with her parents. I always got along fine with Don and Eileen Whitehouse, but I guess—just like anyone would—they had their suspicions when I suddenly re-appeared in Jodie's life. She leans with her hip against the sofa and I beckon her over.

She struts over and her gait is not entirely straight. It doesn't matter. I want to tell her now.

"Let's go out back for a minute," I say.

She cocks her head as if to ask 'Really? You want to fuck me now?'

"I need to ask you something important."

"How sneaky to wait until after I've said 'I do'."

She puts her hand in mine and I guide us to the back patio. She leans into me immediately, her lips on my neck.

"I'm serious, Jodes." I let my fingers run through her hair briefly anyway.

"Okay. I'm all ears." She backs away from me a little, but I can still smell her perfume.

"I've been thinking about this for a while…" I gaze into Jodie's green eyes. "I was wondering if you would be willing to consider me adopting Rosie. So she can have two parents."

Jodie's eyes widen. "For real?"

I nod. "I would hardly joke about that." I recall the time Troy called me Mom and my stunted reaction to that. It's certainly not that I suddenly believe that motherhood is my true calling and any life without it is incomplete. "I love Rosie, and I think it would be advantageous to cover all legal bases."

"I'm not saying no, Leigh, but you are springing this on me… and, truth be told, I'm rather tipsy."

"I felt it was important to ask you today."

"All legal bases, huh…"

Perhaps I could have phrased that better. "I don't want you to be the only one she yells at when she reaches the rebellious stages of puberty."

Jodie chuckles. "How about we continue this conversation tomorrow."

"Agreed." I tug her toward me again. "Mrs. Sterling."

She looks up at me. I'm just joking. We're both keeping our names just the way they are. "I honestly have no idea what ever possessed me to take Gerald's name. Back then, it was just the obvious thing to do, I guess, but in hindsight it seems so ludicrous."

I nod my agreement. "Now," I whisper, "I believe I see a wall with your name on it."

"Just kiss me," she says, and I do.

ACKNOWLEDGMENTS

Endless gratitude to my wife Caroline for supplying the idea for this novel, for always listening patiently to my crazy plans, and for being my partner in just about everything. To Maria for the unwavering enthusiasm when it comes to my stories and for the invaluable beta-reader essays. To Cheyenne Blue for being a stellar, honest editor and an equally excellent friend. To my readers, without whom all of this wouldn't be possible.

Thank you.

ABOUT THE AUTHOR

Harper Bliss is the author of the *Pink Bean* series, the *High Rise* series, the *French Kissing* serial and many other lesbian romance titles. She is the co-founder of Ladylit Publishing and My LesFic weekly newsletter.

Harper loves hearing from readers and you can get in touch with her here:

> www.harperbliss.com
> harper@harperbliss.com

Printed in Great Britain
by Amazon